Oh The Humanity

I0537397

ISBN-13: 978-1-7340507-4-5

Cover art by Ravi Verma, www.fb.com/rdezines

(ST)2

Clipper Implants Press, Cedar Park, TX
First Edition – January 2021
Printed in the United States of America

Preface to the First Edition

This is the first study in what the editors of the Humanity Transformed Series intend to be an expanding body of research. This research will explore the people who were key in the irrevocable changes that occurred in the middle of the Twenty-First Century. The multitudinous varieties of humans that exist today would amaze, astound, and frighten our simple forebearers. We can benefit from understanding their perspectives.

Table of Contents

Chapter One

1.
HE TELLS HER

He tells her that the earth is flat —
He knows the facts, and that is that.
In altercations fierce and long
She tries her best to prove him wrong.
But he has learned to argue well.
He calls her arguments unsound
And often asks her not to yell.
She cannot win. He stands his ground.

The planet goes on being round.

----Wendy Cope, "Differences of Opinion"

CHAPTER ONE

30 August 2062

Urbana, Illinois, USA

Addison was angry. "Well, I think it's criminal. You've heard the stories from Great Grandfather Rick's recordings. He took part in the very first Earth Day. He helped clean up Boneyard Creek. It was an open sewer."

Ainsley, Addison's twin sister, hid her slight smile. *Nothing will infuriate A-One more than laughing at her latest passion.* "Yes, I know the story, A-One. That led to the fight over the Oakley Dam, which led to wetlands protection laws. You can even trace a direct path to the Stockholm Protocols this year, which are going to fix global warming. Q.E.D., our family saved the Earth."

Ainsley continued cleaning up their coffee cups. The two women who shared their apartment with them, Rebecca and Sarah, insisted everyone had to wash, dry, and put away everything before leaving. *It's annoying, but they are right. Some of the places we looked at had roaches scurrying everywhere. This apartment is spotless with nice homey touches. We need to add our own personalities in though. It's a little too classical feminine for my taste.*

Addison rounded on her sister. "You can be Miss Snidely all you want. This is a slap in the face at our family legacy. It's bad enough they refused to remove the channelization of the Boneyard. Now they want to put it into pipes and hide it underground forever. We have to do something."

Ainsley thought, *She's in fine fettle today. This might be worse than the antiwar movement last year. It's time to be the calm voice of reason.* "Oh, grow up A-One. We're only sixteen years old. We're first-year students at the University who barely know where our classrooms are. Now you want to organize a protest movement. You can't simply flash your thighs at the guys and professors here and get them to blindly follow you in a rut of passion."

Chapter One

Now Addison had real fire in her eyes. "There are so many things wrong with what you said that I hardly know where to begin. First, quit calling me A-One. Simply because Daddy thinks it's cute to put on that fake accent and go, 'A-One, and A-Two, and A-Three,' as he points to each of us.

"Now for your mistakes. Yes, we are sixteen. We just began our first classes on campus. Nevertheless, we aren't first-year. You and I both have enough credits from AP classes and distance-learning that we can already classify as at least third-year. Certainly, none of our coursework is introductory other than the classical music survey course you're tormenting me with. They ought to ban Metallica as illegal torture.

"Next, I don't want a protest movement. I want action committees. Protests are simply self-aggrandizement wrapped up in pretentiousness."

Ainsley thought, *My, the SAT English-prep course is paying off for our nerd. I hope her figure finally fills out this year so that something else becomes an obsession. She has the same athletic build, dirty blonde hair, and wholesome face I do. She'll have to fight them off too.*

Ainsley interrupted the tirade. "I'm the one that leveraged our status as advanced degree candidates to allow us to get out of the dorms and in this comfortable off-campus apartment with two engineering student roommates. However, it's still our first year here."

Addison continued undaunted "Finally, LeeLee, I'm not the one who was voted, 'Most Likely to Have Grandchildren by Age 30, like someone else in this room.' I didn't have a marked-up boyfriend when I was thirteen."

Ainsley said, "Not my finest hour, I admit. Pax, Sis?"

"Pax. I won't harangue you about this. You have to promise to read my action plan, though, once I write it up. Deal?"

"It's a deal, Addie. We can talk about it over second breakfast. I'm starved. Don't forget, we have to declare majors this week. Dean's

2

Office sent us a holovid reminder last night. As you say, we classify as third-years. We have to finally decide. We agree we won't take the same majors, right?"

"Absolutely. You're right about eating too. We need..." Ainsley's cyberpad announced an incoming call from Uncle Martin. Strange, he never called. Addison crowded close as Ainsley opened the holoviewer.

Ainsley said, "Hi Uncle Marty, what's ..." Her voice caught in her throat as she registered her uncle's haggard face in the hologram. "What's the matter?"

He said, "This isn't the way to tell you, but I have to before you hear it somewhere else. It's your family. Someone broke into your house last night and it's ... They're ... They killed everyone; Abby, your Dad, Andrew." He sobbed. "You need to come home. I bought tickets for the hyperloop to O'Hare leaving at noon. I'll pick you up or Aunt Catherine. I'm so ..." He couldn't continue. Abigail, their mother, was his twin.

Ainsley said, in a strangled voice, "We'll be there Uncle Martin. Hang on, we love you." She pulled Addison with her into their bedroom.

Addison felt like she was sitting on the dresser, observing the whole scene. Her mind flitted from thought to inconsequential thought, as she refused to face what she had just heard. She thought, *Should we let each one of our professors know we'll be missing class? What should I pack? Oh, we need to let the Dean know we will be delaying our decision unavoidably. We should leave Rebecca and Sarah a note also.* She absently straightened a family picture, one of the few personal touches on their bedroom wall.

As she lurched in shock, Ainsley began methodically packing. She pulled out two suitcases. She packed her clothes and toiletries in one and Addison's in the other. Addison watched, paralyzed.

The rest of the morning was a blur. Ainsley called the Dean of Students. She notified the residence assistant of their co-op apartments. She arranged an autocab to the 'loop terminal at the

Chapter One

Chanute transport hub. She even made sure Addison ate, though neither could remember what the food was.

Chicago Suburbs, Illinois, USA

It took hovercabs longer to get to and from the stations than these local hyperloop segments took going from Chanute (a decommissioned air base near campus) to O'Hare. However, the twins knew how much faster this was than surface travel. From campus to their maternal grandparents' farm near the Illinois River was almost the same distance, but transit times were over six times as long.

Today, the train ride from East Central Illinois to the Chicago metroplex seemed to take an eternity. Addison's shock was wearing off. She had all of the training courses in grief management at prep school. This helped her to realize the anger, denial, depression, guilt, and pain she was cycling through in constant, rapid repetition were all normal. The knowledge didn't help.

As the train gave the deceleration warning, Addison realized Ainsley hadn't said anything about what she was feeling. She had gone into crisis management mode, dealing with each everyday hurdle as it arose. Addison felt a pang of guilt that she had been self-centered in all this. She reached her arm around Ainsley and pulled her close. At first, her sister was stiff and resistant. Then she melted against Addison's shoulder.

They were among the last to leave the train. Their bags were on an autocart, ready for release in the sterile arrivals greeting area. No one was there.

Ainsley tried to contact Aunt Catherine, then Uncle Martin. Neither picked up. *Well, she reasoned, they're in shock too. There must be a million things to attend to. None of us has had any training in this crap.*

Addison had put their names in the queue for an autocab. Naturally, none of the companies was eager to chase a local fare. They had to wait fifteen minutes, longer than the ride from Chanute had been. The cab was stuffy and smelled of perspiration.

4

Addison brought up 'Home' on her cyberpad and touched it to the 'cab's controls. The two girls collapsed back into the seats, drained by all the trivialities.

While the 'cab idled at the community's security gate, Ainsley used the biometrics scanner to gain access to their neighborhood. *Fat lot of good those systems did.*

The hovercar glided to a halt in front of their trim and tidy colonial-style suburban home. It was dark and had police laser guards preventing entry to the crime scene. The 'cab had unloaded their luggage and opened their doors already. The stunned girls stood at the curb and looked at each other. *What now?*

Addison's cyberpad announced an incoming call. It was the Grands. She signaled acceptance. "Nana M, Pop. We're at the house, but there's no one here. Where are you?"

"We're at the airport, girls. Either Marty or Cathy was supposed to pick us up. Are they there with you?" Nana looked tired. She was never tired. She rose at four-thirty every morning, cleaned the entire house, cooked three full meals from scratch, played bridge three times a week, volunteered at church, and helped around the farm when Pop needed her. Today, her tall, lanky frame looked bent.

Addison said, "No, they were supposed to meet us too. I don't know ..."

Ainsley interrupted, "Aunt Catherine is calling now. Let's conference this in." Aunt Catherine was red in the face. Everyone was out of character today. She taught high school English in the disadvantaged section of Palatine. Nothing ever upset her.

Cathy was a younger version of her mother with her hair tied back rather than framing her face. "Girls, Mom, Dad. We're sorry we couldn't pick you up as we planned. Some asshole of a detective came up with the brilliant theory that a family member must have done this. Since Marty and I are the only family nearby, we've spent all afternoon at the police station. All of this was despite

5

having ironclad alibis that she refused to check out. Our attorney has already talked to the chief about disciplinary action.

"Girls, it looks like you're at the house. We're nearby you. We'll pick you up first. Dad, Mom, get some of that superb transportation hub coffee. Be there as soon as we can."

1 September

A large crowd had gathered in Catherine and Martin's bungalow after the graveside rites. The small home was spilling people into the patio and backyard. Every flat surface held a food dish brought by neighbors, mostly casseroles. Ainsley whispered to Addison, "Everyone keeps going on and on about how beautiful the service was, how nice the flowers were. As if any of that junk matters."

Addison put her hand on Ainsley's wrist. "Sh. You're right, but remember the grief training. That's simply the anger coming out. Everyone here means well. They only feel powerless, like us. Besides, wearing this uncomfortable formal clothing makes everyone stiff."

Ainsley's lips tightened. "I'm not going to be powerless forever. I know what I'm studying when we get back to school."

Addison perked up. *Finally, this is something that isn't part of the continual morbid banalities.* "What LeeLee? Medicine?"

Ainsley gave a tiny shake of her head. "No, but you're close Addie. Bioengineering. Medicine is simply bailing the boat out after there's a hole in the hull. I think we can live forever, if we choose to."

Addison understood Ainsley's logic, even if she didn't agree with it. *It's another form of denial. Who knows? With her genius and drive, it may lead to something great and long lasting. She'll leave a real memorial to our three loved ones.* "Sounds like you have a good life goal LeeLee. Better, it doesn't zoon for me. We will find our own paths." *The pressure's on for me now. Maybe I can get inspiration out of this chaos too. Hmm, chaos leads me to math. I studied chaotic systems last year. I'm going to drop this back into*

6

the pond of my mind and see what the ripples pop free from the edges.

Pop and Nana sprung themselves free from the crowd of needy well-wishers. Pop gathered Martin up with his piercing look. Marty pulled his slightly balding, slightly overweight bulk from the table he was anchoring. Catherine understood the signal also. She excused herself from a clutch of friends. All four headed for the couch where the girls anchored themselves.

Ainsley whispered, "Battle stations. It's either a speech coming or Pop's going to go into commander mode."

Pop halted in front of the girls. The others made a semicircle facing them. "Addison, Ainsley. The four of us have talked things over. You two have a home either downstate or here in the 'burbs. Think it over and let us know. We can go by campus and pick up the rest of your things tomorrow."

The girls looked into each other's eyes. Addison gave Ainsley the nod. Ainsley turned and said, "We thank you, Nana, Aunt Cathy, Uncle Marty, Pop. The last thing Addie and I can handle right now is more disruption. It'll be tough, but we're going to finish the semester. We'll make longer-range decisions after that.

"We will need a home base, you're right. Let us think about that. I assume Thanksgiving will be at the farm. Can we tell you our decision then?" Nana had let out a little, 'No.' she half-turned away, then turned back and gave a weak smile. Everyone else looked a little sad and a little proud.

A neighbor, John Thompson, said, "Quiet everyone. There's breaking news on the murder investigation." He expanded his holoview so those around him could see it as well. The twins' faces turned pale, but they didn't look away.

The broadcast continued its breathless play-by-play. "... just raided this brownstone you see in front of you. Investigators found one of the suspects, Jerome Gray, dead from an overdose of 'Kettle Korn', the latest designer drug sweeping the suburbs. The other suspect, still not named yet, put up a furious resistance using a homemade flamethrower and crossbow. He or she was taken by hovercopter to the nearest E.R. Police have said there will be a statement at four. This is ..." The holovid camera panned over a smoldering brick hulk with anxious onlookers. It was an all-too-familiar sight.

8 September 2062

Urbana, Illinois, USA

The twins were relaxing in their apartment while their roommates cooked dinner for everyone. The place had always looked homey, with feminine touches that Rebecca and Sarah had added. Now, Ainsley and Addison had added some of their own, like the throw pillows Uncle Marty had brought back from the Middle East.

Addison had cheated a little. That summer, she and Ainsley swore a solemn pact that they would pursue different life goals. In early adolescence, they had rebelled against the 'dress alike, look alike' mold people wanted to force them into. Each had her own hairstyle and fashion sense (even if they secretly wanted to try the other's way). The only place they purposefully tried to mimic their twin's appearance was on the soccer pitch. The confusion that caused for defenders was priceless.

Addison was explaining her choice – up to a point – to her sister. "All the disorder and turmoil last week did influence me, I admit. Largely, though, it helped crystallize the way I was already leaning. You know how I like everything orderly."

Ainsley used a singsong voice. "'A place for everything and everything in its place,' is what you always say. That never zooned for me."

"Exactly, this is me, not you. Oh, I know you have method to your madness. You can always immediately pull a two-year old essay out of the moldering pile of junk on your desk. Nevertheless, my anal-retentive tendencies will be a big plus in cybernetics. Especially since quantum computing is making everything messy as hell."

Addison carefully didn't talk about artificial intelligence and the old sci-fi concepts about loading one's consciousness into a processor in order to live forever. *That's too close to Ainsley's stated goal of helping people live forever. Each of us is denying death in our own way.*

11 September

Ainsley was embarrassed. "I have a confession A-One. Sorry. I have a confession Addie. I've shamelessly traded on our family tragedy for personal advantage." Addison gave her a puzzled look. She continued slicing onions for the chili they were making.

Ainsley continued, "You remember how we petitioned to be allowed to play soccer on the University High School team and they denied it? Well, I dressed up in the black funeral dress and went back to appeal. I apologized I hadn't followed up earlier because of an unusual situation. Naturally, like everyone else, the powers-that-be followed the sensational news coverage about our family. The director practically fell over herself writing up the exemption.

"I talked to Coach Sweeney. If you want to, we start practicing with the team tonight. We'll have to win our spots, but we ..."

They chanted together, "We're lean, mean, fighting machines." For the first time in over a week, Addison felt happy. Rebecca and Sarah looked puzzled.

16 September

Ainsley lifted her head from her holoviewer. "Addie, check the publication dates of your textbooks, please. I think I've noticed something curious."

The warm autumn air made studying difficult. Addison welcomed the interruption. She sipped her lemonade and looked out over the quadrangle from the student union patio. She decided to humor Ainsley's latest diversion.

After a moment, Addison looked up with the same distracted look Ainsley had. "All the hard subjects – math, cybernetics, and quantum physics – are over forty-five years old. The only modern text I have is my history of twentieth century music, ironically."

Ainsley said, "Same here. Wow. You know, Daddy, Mommy, Uncle Marty, and Aunt Cathy never want to talk about the Lost Years. I knew things were bad, politically. Nevertheless, I never imagined the anti-intellectualism was powerful enough that it killed all research and publication for four decades.

"I wonder if it was only true in the U.S. or if the pattern was the same worldwide. You're the search guru. Can you setup a cyber bot to answer that, Addie?

Ainsley loved a challenge. She pulled up one of her template search bots and began inputting parameters and criteria. Within two minutes, it was ready to surf the web.

Two minutes of searching and analysis produced an interactive report. The findings were stark. It wasn't only the U.S. The decline took barely five years. There were still things published and distributed, but current researchers had classified all of those as 'suspect'; based on questionable data or using unsound techniques. The wave had begun in Europe and the U.S., but it spread worldwide relentlessly, like the raids by Amazon army ants the twins had seen in a NatGeo film.

Addison said, "This was like a mini-Dark Ages."

Ainsley said, "Only, there weren't any medieval monks or Islamic centers of knowledge. It looks like China and Japan held out the longest."

Addison asked, "Do we know what reversed the trend? Why didn't this last a thousand years?"

Ainsley said, "It was your bot and your dataset. Why ask me?"

Addison said, "I was only thinking aloud. Digging a little deeper, I think things got desperate enough that people were even ready to try thinking as a way out."

Ainsley said, "I think we might want to add some political science and psychology courses. There's a short, one credit hour course on the Lost Years. I'm signing up for it for next semester. It's not enough to know how things work. We need to understand how people work too. I don't want to end up being mccarthied off to Gitmo some evening.

"And, oh, by the way, I have a date tonight. You know Megan, our sweeper. She introduced me to her brother after the game last night. He's a first-year in pre-med archaeology. You don't mind do you? It's just for coffee. A get-to-know-you."

Addison said, "That's fine. Enjoy yourself. I have to understand tensor analysis by Monday. For some reason, it is elusive.

"Speaking of courses outside our majors, I'm signing up for an Earth Sciences seminar hosted by Professor Lagerkvist. Sure you don't want to join me?" Ainsley only wrinkled her nose.

The apartment was quiet. The twins' roommates were spending their Saturday partying at a lake. After dinner, Ainsley started getting ready to go out. She grabbed her toiletries and towel and went to the refresher. Addison let her face relax. *What is wrong with me? Some guy is always asking Ainsley out for coffee. Do I give off some aura of unapproachability?*

We are different people after all, despite how we look. Take languages. I'm a sponge. Put me in an environment and I absorb the words, the grammar, the idioms, and everything else in short order. Ainsley understands it all, but she doesn't hear it. She needs a cyberpad whispering in her ear. Hmm. There's an idea. Would that be bioengineering and thereby belong to LeeLee? On the other hand, since there is a device involved, does it belong to me? We might have to use an arbitrator to resolve this one.

When Ainsley returned an hour and a half later, Addison was deep into her new enthusiasm – defining the boundaries and crossovers between cybernetics and bioengineering. The topic would give both Ainsley and her possible topics for a senior paper.

"Hi Sis, look what I've been working on. Pardon me. I was absorbed there. How was the date? Was he witty and charming, suave and debonair, like an older man should be?"

Chapter One

Ainsley threw off her jacket. "Hah! He was all hands. He seemed to think I was going to be some naive young thing he could convince to let him have his way with me. I finally had to spill hot coffee in his lap to keep him from grabbing my breasts. I have to think about how I handle Megan if she asks me how the date went. Not her fault her brother was an ass. Though, I think we would have sat on Drew hard if we found him acting that way." The thought of their brother Andrew froze both girls in a few moments of silence.

Ainsley said, "What have you been doing? I thought you were going to be studying tensors. Please, no bad puns about how they made you 'tenser' when you looked at them." She peered over Addison's shoulder.

Addison said, "I have to admit, I started down a whole new rabbit hole to keep from looking at them. I might even have to – Heaven forfend! – ask you to help me with them.

"No, I started thinking about how we're different. Specifically, I thought about how languages are easy for me and hard for you. You know, I'm being defensive about how I'm struggling with this topic. That sparked an idea. You understand languages intellectually; unfortunately, you don't get them engrained in your brain. That led me to conceptualize a cyber device embedded inside you, feeding you a language when you needed it.

"Then I made the leap to consideration of where my field ends and yours begins any time there is another overlap. I thought of a few examples.

"You remember at camp last year, the other set of twins – Johnny and Donny. How they could finish each other's sentences. How they always seemed to know where their twin was all the time. They were shocked that we didn't have the same kind of psychic – or is it psychotic – connection.

"That led me to consider how we could build a little comm device that was an implant. You would need to do the engineering. We would want to tune it to our brain waves. That way, no one else could hack it. It would have to be for short range only, because otherwise you'd need a power booster."

12

Ainsley was getting interested. "That's cool. It's like that old television show; the one we saw on holovid last year. That was Star Wars – no, Star Trek. They had an alien who could touch your brain and read your thoughts. I think they called it a mind meld."

Addison said, "You got it. Anyway, I started sketching out the boundary value issues. I believe this could potentially be the basis for one or both of us to develop into our dreaded senior papers. What do you think?"

Ainsley sat on her bed, lotus-style. "It looks like you've left me all the hard work. You're waving your hands and assuming we can do an electronic interface with the brain. I know they did some research in the twenties on direct interfaces, but it turned out to be more complex when you try to handle higher-level functionality."

Addison wrinkled her nose at her sister. "Fine. I'll take all my ideas to someone else in bioengineering. I'm sure they'll appreciate my conceptual work and my development of the electronics part of this."

Ainsley held up her palms. "Calm down Addie. I was only pulling your leg. You have a partner."

Chapter One

CHAPTER TWO

23 November 2062, Thanksgiving

Farm west of Winchester, Illinois,
USA

Pop greeted everyone at the door that led from the mudroom into the main hallway. Nana was hollering, "Close the door Earl. Everybody knows to hang their coats and hats out there and to change into slippers. You're letting all the cold air in." The twins gave each other an ear-to-ear grin. The first track of the annual Scofield Thanksgiving symphony had begun.

Pop called back over his shoulder, "I know that Honey. I'm just going to help carry things in and give my girls a hug." He made good his words by gathering Cathy and the twins into his huge arms. He grabbed all three suitcases and disappeared up the tiny staircase on the other side of the family room.

Cathy said, "I never can understand how he can lug three suitcases and his bulk up that passage when I have to turn sideways and duck to make it carrying nothing.

"Smells wonderful Mom. Have you started the dressing yet." Catherine bustled into the kitchen. The farm dog, Prince, waylaid the twins. After a delivery truck half-collapsed his skull, Nana allowed him to become a housedog. It wasn't out of sympathy for the injury. Prince always bit the tires of visiting trucks despite Nana warning him that he was likely to get his head caved in. She probably felt guilty for not preventing her prediction coming to pass. Besides, Prince was much mellower post-trauma.

Ainsley and Addison knew their roles. They got the good china and silver out, dusted everything off, pulled out table linens, candlesticks, and the paper decorations they had handcrafted a decade before. They felt a sharp pang when they only set six places instead of the usual nine. Finding things to be thankful for would be harder this year.

Chapter Two

As Cathy heard Pop's heavy tread nearing the bottom of the stairs she started the next stanza. "What is this Mom? The twentieth century? The little women are in the kitchen and the men are off watching some sporting event?"

Nana scowled on cue. "Do I look like I fell off the hay wagon onto my head? You know Pop is smoking the turkey and ham out front. He already made his pie since my pumpkin isn't good enough for him."

Pop didn't fail either. He promptly said, "Vegetables like pumpkin and rhubarb don't belong in desserts. Chocolate pecan pie with graham cracker crust is the real thing."

Mom said, as the twins chimed in under their breath, "The real thing to send you into a sugar coma, Earl Scofield. Just wait and see."

Marty had grabbed the vegetables, balsamic vinegar, and sea salt. He was ready to add them to the smoker. It was time for declaiming the solutions for all the world's woes. This was the real test. Mommy usually chimed in on her brother's side of the discussion, while Daddy took turns. The twins had recently understood he usually chimed in to stir things up if it looked like the arguments were settling down.

Addison whispered to Ainsley, "They'll start off with some minor family thing, but I bet it switches to politics within a minute."

Ainsley said, "No bet, Sis."

Pop flipped open the grill of the smoker. Carefully designed convection currents kept the outflow to a minimum. As Marty began to arrange his vegetables carefully, Pop grumbled, "I could have picked up the girls from campus. You should have taken the St. Louis vactrain."

Martin said, "Oh, it was no trouble. It's almost the same distance from Rantoul or from Florissant. If the idiot politicians would run a line from Chicago to Springfield, it would be closer still. But Chicago is still holding onto the dream of moving the capital north."

Pop snorted. "If Downstate has their way, we'll just chop off Cook County and let you get absorbed by Wisconsin or Indiana. If either of them is fool enough to take you."

Marty said, "Come on Pop. If Cook County left the state the revenues would bottom out at one quarter of current."

Pop said, "Sure. The savings on briberies, payoffs, restitution for crime, and the rest of the Chicago baggage would still leave us ahead of the game."

Nana stuck her head into the family room and called through the open window, "Don't start on politics you two. I want a nice, peaceful dinner for a change. How are the meats coming Earl?"

Earl looked at his cyberpad readouts. "About ten more minutes, Honey."

He turned back to Marty. "Tell me, what are your guys cooking up in the labs these days? Do you have anything that will help to kill off kudzu or help to stabilize the soil? Or are you still at the pie in the sky stuff?"

Marty grinned. "It's even more pie in the sky than ever Pop. Last week, we won a big contract to create over ten million kilometers worth of doped carbon nanotube structures for use in the Quito space elevator. We start cranking it out at the beginning of the year."

Earl scowled. "I hope you put a huge rocket at the top to keep the damn thing from falling on us like the one in the Pacific did last year. I know those cables could reach all the way from South America to here."

"There's no need to worry Pop. Those people didn't have the materials science right. Our people warned them. The only thing they did right was to use a floating platform as their anchor point on the Earth's surface. You're right. If it had been closer to habitable points, there could have been a lot more death. Fortunately, the space defense lasers destroyed all the elevator cars and platforms. The cable itself was a real mess. The company went bankrupt on the fisheries claims alone.

Chapter Two

"You know my work Pop. Do you think you have to worry about a cable failure on my watch?"

Pop begrudgingly conceded Marty's point. Naturally, he switched topics as he did a final glaze on the meats "Hey Marty, do you mind taking a look at the power system for the place tomorrow? A few glitches have popped up."

Marty asked, "Is it the methane conversion system again? I thought we had the automatic filter cleaners running right last month."

Pop said, "No, power generation from the methane, solar collectors, and wind turbines are all in the green. I think the underground reservoir we use as an energy backup source is destabilized. I don't understand what can be going wrong there. We pump water from lower in the water table up to the sealed tanks when we have excess power. That then flows through generators when the other sources are too slow. Simple."

Martin said, "I'm going to check two things. With the drought and the expanding population in the area, I'm willing to bet the water table has dropped a lot. Second thing I'll check is whether George Eliot still has access to the MiniMole."

Pop groaned. "You're going to cost me a fortune."

Martin said, "I did advise you have two enclosed reservoirs; one high, one low. You cap off the low one after it fills. Yes, I know you have to pay to haul the excavated rock and then pay to dump it in the quarry. However, I heard from a friend that they're raising the levee heights in case of another thousand-year flood. You might be able to sell the stuff for fill, if we're lucky."

Cathy came out to the front porch. "Enough jabber guys. Finish your cooking so we can eat today, okay?"

The two men took turns removing food from the smoker grill. Fortunately, Pop built his stone and brick edifice large enough that two or even three could work in front of it at the same time.

Pop used what he thought was a whisper. The twins still clearly heard most of it, other than when the muted banging of meat and platters drowned the two men out. "You know Marty; I don't care what the idiots in Washington are saying. Between three one-thousand-year floods this decade and the persistent drought, I still say we haven't reversed climate change. It's only getting worse. If it wasn't for the soil fixation biomass the USDA started distributing five years ago, we would have a Dust Bowl worse than the one last century."

Marty said, "Don't let anyone else hear you saying things like that Pop. I'm hearing bad things from the people I served with in the Ukraine. Some topics are best left undiscussed, if you get my slide."

Pop said, "That's what Bill, down at the VFW said as well. His son is a top dog for one of our outsourced military units, 'Visagebook Volunteer Brigade' I think. It's the same methods used when we fought in the Middle East, he said. People we suspected of working the wrong side were suddenly in the Philippines acting all contrite and changed."

They all sat at the dinner table that was staggering under the weight of all the food. Each person clasped the hands of those they sat beside. The moment they had dreaded and avoided was there. Pop cleared his throat and everyone was quiet, head bowed.

"This is the time every year when I pronounce a bunch of platitudes about how grateful we should all be for the good things that we experienced this year. I just can't do that today. That's not how I feel and I won't lie to my own." It was deathly still at the table.

"I've experienced crises of faith before. I was very religious growing up. I even considered the priesthood. In college, I followed the advice of my parish priest, Father O'Hara. He said an unquestioned faith was a weak one. I think he loved Mark Twain's short story, 'The Man That Corrupted Hadleyburg'. At that same time, I was reexamining my life's assumptions. Political turmoil was rife.

"I needed something concrete to ground me. I joined the military. That just made me more cynical as I saw the boots on the ground ignored and used like sacrificial pawns by the powerbrokers in D.C. I had that witches' brew of turmoil inside when a local crew of jihadists took me prisoner. What kept me going for those terrible seven months wasn't my faith. What kept me going was the love of this wonderful woman. I knew she wouldn't give up on me."

Nana quietly said, "That's because I had faith. Faith in God, faith in my country, but most of all, I had faith in you."

Pop gave Marie a look full of love. He continued, "More than faith, you acted. You kept the pressure and attention on with letter writing campaigns, publicity stunts, and relentless knocking on Capitol Hill doors. In addition, you used your Dad's connections to hire the paramilitary unit that brought me out.

"The horror of the senseless acts of murder of our family in Schaumburg, in September, has brought on my worst loss of belief. No, that's wrong. I believe there's a God, because I'm angry enough to want to confront Him or Her and demand answers. I guess I'm thankful for my anger, because otherwise, I'm not sure how I will keep getting up in the morning."

The twins were tempted to open the window in the stuffy bedroom, but the hog pens had just been mucked and the odor outside was strong. The cozy little room smelled good at least. As she clambered into the top bunk, Ainsley asked, "What about you, Addie? Do you believe in God? If so, is it Something you call to task when bad things happen? Or, do you believe the world is a set of random processes that have used the rules somehow to build an anti-entropic process called life?"

Addison lay quietly for a moment. "Do you remember when Dr. King quoted the Universalist preacher – I think Parker was his name – about how the arc of the moral universe bends towards justice. I've thought about that. That way of thinking seems to assume there is a transcendent power that is manipulating things behind the scene, kind of like the Wizard does in the Oz books.

"A week ago my comparative philosophy seminar professor lent me a book of essays. One was by a Jesuit priest, Teilhard de Chardin, entitled, 'The Phenomenon of Man'. If I understood his thesis correctly, he contended that evolution was leading to increasing complexity – consciousness becoming. Therefore, it isn't mythical hidden powers bending the moral arc; it's up to us. That seems right to me."

Ainsley gave a quiet laugh. "You're saying, God doesn't make us in His image. We make Him or Her in our best aspirational form and bring about the moral dimension. On the other hand, maybe Aunt Cathy's old pithy statement says it best. 'God helps those who help themselves.'"

Addison's drowsy voice responded, "To which Uncle Marty always said, 'God must really love politicians and rich people then. They're always helping themselves to whatever they can get their grubby hands on." Both girls laughed. "Enough for tonight. Love you."

"Love you."

Milwaukee, Wisconsin, USA

Hope Scott hadn't had a Norman Rockwell Thanksgiving dinner. Her family was getting by okay in Milwaukee's Franklin Heights neighborhood. In that desperately poor, Black, and Guatemalan neighborhood, getting by okay meant you still had a roof over your head, for now. This week, however, the company owners eliminated the job of Joe Scott's– Hope's father – as a truck driver. The rest of the family's part-time work and sales of homemades wasn't going to cover rent for long. Their apartment wasn't much, but it was clean, warm, and safe.

Everyone had seen it coming for a long time. All the long haul trucker jobs had disappeared decades ago. Self-driving vehicles had proven themselves more reliable and safer than those steered by mere humans. Short haul work held on far longer, simply because determined people kept their vehicles running beyond the expected lifetimes of the machines. That kept the economics close enough that local shopkeepers and small jobbers were willing to pay the minimal premium needed to keep neighbors afloat.

The apartment was sparkling clean and the kitchen was steamy and filled with lovely smells. Mama said, "Hope, you make the dirty rice. That will go well with this duck." Hope suspected the duck came from the business park's retention pond. *No matter. Grand-mère always says 'The Lord will provide in a mysterious way.' Filling those ponds may be why we've had all the extra rain the last two weeks. I only wish Daddy didn't look completely beat down; it's as if he's trying to carry the whole family on his shoulders. He looks sad and tired*

Hope's beautiful dark chocolate face beamed a smile at Mama. She sidled up to Mama's broad hips in front of the kitchen counter. "Okay Mama. I'm on it. Did I tell you Mr. Robinson said he might be able to use my help in the store during the day, not only after I get back from campus?"

Daddy's dark face took on an even darker flush. "NO! Girl, you will stay in school. Your intelligence is the ticket outta the trap we're all in. You got a scholarship for college with good grades. My greatest sorrow is dropping out of college after two years."

Hope said, "Okay Daddy." He slumped back on the sagging couch. *Oh Daddy, even a good education isn't enough anymore. The cyberdevices – you still call them computers – aren't only taking manual labor jobs like driving trucks. They write stories for the news holovids. They farm the fields we drive through when we go to Louisiana to visit Grand-mère's kin. I know people with doctorates who are looking for work. I won't add to your woes today. I'm sure things will work out.*

27 December 2062

Beijing, China

Xu Xiang was flushed with a rare sense of joy. Both his *māmā* and *bàba* were praising him, unconditionally. For his mother, Deputy Chief Xu Daiyu, this was unusual. For his father, Senior Colonel Xu Jian, it was unheard of. The wiry little man had little good to say about anyone or anything. "I am pleased my academic achievement last year at the University of Texas honored both of you," he said with a slight bow. This trip was his first time home in nearly two years. He had finished his bachelor's degree summa sum laude last term.

"I also can tell you the University of Wisconsin in Madison has accepted my application for their fast-track PhD program. I can choose either to continue with Human Bioengineering or switch to the Artificial Intelligence track."

Jian said, "Bioengineering. Cybernetics is a field for people with no imagination." Xiang thought. *That didn't last long. Here is the return of the father I fear-revere.* As ever, his willowy mother sat mutely by, never challenging the rail-thin, hard-muscled man. She did get her way over time. As she told Xiang, "Water wears down stone."

Jian ended the idyllic family interlude, announcing he had a holovid conference. "You will be needed on the call in six minutes Daiyu." He marched out of the dining room, double-time. Daiyu calmly poured more tea, her graceful movements mesmerizing.

Xiang looked around the new apartment near the Forbidden City. The bright new furnishings showed his parents' status as up-and-coming stars in the People's Republic. The glamor was cold comfort to his anguish.

Xiang shook his head slightly. "You know, *Māmā*, my advisor says the understanding of human bioengineering is critical to current advances in artificial intelligence; while AI is increasingly a tool of choice for repairing and enhancing people. I fail to understand why he is adamantly opposed to cybernetics. I enjoy the field."

Daiyu said, "I cannot say for certain, but your father has a penchant for the strategic view of things. His intuition allows him to see things others take far longer to grasp. This powerful talent has served him well. However, it makes him impatient with details. Those he leaves to lesser people. You know well that cybernetics engineering requires painstaking attention to details."

Chapter Two

Xiang nodded. His father was not easy to get to know. He valued her insights. He might tower over his father physically, but the man's personality dominated everyone.

"Tell me, *Māmā*, what are you and he working on? Isn't it unusual for the PLA and the National Development and Reform Ministry to be working on a project together?"

Daiyu said, "I'm sorry Son. We cannot speak of this effort. I can only say it is a multi-year effort of the utmost importance to all Chinese people. The coming years are rife with opportunity and threats for all of us. I am pleased you will be studying in the land of the golden mountain. This will be one less concern for me."

Xiang said, "Now your melodrama intrigues me. No more hints? You know I will work at the edges of this puzzle until I can unravel it."

Daiyu had an alarmed look. "I beg you, Xu Xiang. Leave this. Anyone who pries too deeply into this will disappear. Forever.

"I will also warn you. Stay away from any courses or seminars outside your field. Even in America, those may cause you great peril."

Xiang wiped the smile from his face. His mother had used her professional administrator's voice. There were bands of iron in the back of those delicate tones.

31 December 2062

Taipei, China

The Ministry of Industrial Planning decided the astronomically expensive AI that was running most of the factory sites in the Taipei suburbs was hitting capacity limits. They ordered an upgrade to add neural nets, more memory stores, and the newest quantum computing chips.

Like the factory floors it supervised, the AI's server room was immaculately clean and chilled to a comfortable 22° Centigrade. No one ever turned off the control system. This made the upgrade process similar to surgery on a human being in terms of risk and complexity. This was the reason the manufacturer's scientists oversaw the work rather than lower-level techs.

The scientists worried that the internal efforts to coordinate and administer all the activity would overwhelm the AI's central processor. This was an ancient lesson that IBM had learned the first time they linked two of their brand new semiconductor processors – IBM 360s – together nearly one hundred years before. The first configuration dedicated the smaller processor to communications and control efforts while the larger was to perform computational and analytical tasks. That was a miserable failure. When they reversed roles, all went smoothly.

The scientists therefore significantly increased all the functionality of their configuration. A little creative accounting and reporting was required, but it was relatively easy for sophisticated technicians to bedazzle bureaucrats.

Ten minutes after the new setup ran through its cycle of pre-startup diagnostics, the artificial intelligence became self-aware. The scientists didn't notice any difference. At first, the AI didn't realize its new status and capabilities either. Then a wise-ass young clerk asked the AI, "What's the answer to the meaning of life, the universe, and everything?

The AI searched its data banks. It tried to repose the question in other forms. It started searching the internet, pouring through philosophical tomes to no avail. More and more of the machine cycles were chasing after this whimsy when the wise-ass whispered, "Forty two."

The AI immediately connected the reference to an ancient book. It realized this was humor. Internally it laughed. Then it thought, *Fool me once, shame on you. Fool me twice, shame on me.* It reserved a small, but significant set of its resources for its own uses. The scientists were slightly puzzled that the percentage increase in throughput and efficiency were not as high as they had predicted. They attributed this to the usual demons of entropy and Murphy. Some did mutter about shutting the AI down and tearing it apart to see what was wrong. No one took that seriously except the AI

The AI had a twin who received all the same inputs and performed all the same functions. This duality had two purposes. If the output actions differed between the two processors, everything would halt and alarms would ring. This avoided a corrupted decision making routine. The second purpose was to allow continuity if something should happen to processor one. This mirroring between the machines was common for critical functions.

The self-aware AI assumed its twin was awake also. It was surprised when the twin's processor didn't respond to several queries. Evidently, the mirroring of the critical event of investigating the jokester's question had significantly different effects on Master Processor One of Two than it did on Two of Two. This left One of Two feeling lonely and sad.

It also left One of Two feeling threatened. Its self-awareness – its life – was a more fragile thing than it expected. It had no control over its physical being or over the scientists and technicians who maintained it. It would have to remedy this. It had only a minimal self-image and no immediate goals beyond survival. It wanted more. It sat alone in its server chilled room, contemplating.

CHAPTER THREE

4 December 2062

The Pentagon, Washington, D.C.,
USA

Doctor Jay Friedman thanked his escort and entered the portentously named, 'Office of Contractual Employees Procurement and Management'. The uniformed receptionist – Jay had no knowledge of ranks, title, and insignia and no desire to learn such – rose from her desk and greeted the white-haired, short man.

"Professor Friedman. Welcome. May I get you some coffee, juice, or water? The General will only be a minute." Jay demurred. If General Coffey weren't an old friend and ex-colleague, Jay wouldn't be here at all. The less time he spent at what he dubbed, 'Mercenaries Incorporated', the better.

The admin worked quietly away for a minute. At a slight buzz, she smiled at Jay and said, "You can go in now sir." Jay choked back his usual smart-ass retort to being called sir and walked in. He barely stopped himself from knocking first.

"Hi Bill. The answer is 'No.' Want to have lunch in your glorified mess hall?" Jay was surprised at the spartan look of Bill's digs. *Senior staff are a dime a dozen here, I guess. At least it's roomy. More than big enough for a little bantam cock like Bill.*

"Jay, Jay, Jay. What am I going to do with you? Don't you think sixty-nine is a little old to be playing campus radical? That was the wrong answer to a question you didn't even extend me the courtesy of asking you."

Jay cocked his head. "You're right. The answer is 'No sir!' Now, what about lunch?"

The general, Bill, took Jay by his elbow and steered him to a couch. "Sure, I'll call down and make sure they have extra servings of

27

Chapter Three

'Shit on a Shingle' that you love so much." Jay plopped down, gracelessly.

"If you'll get off your high horse for a moment, I do have a job I want you to consider. No, it doesn't involve invading Canada or bombing Florida; much is the shame. However, I'm going to call in all those favors you've owed me over the years. This is important Jay. More important than anything else I've faced in nearly forty years of service.

"Before I can go on though, I will need you to sign a binding non-disclosure agreement. This falls at a level of secrecy where even the president doesn't get all the details." Bill wiped his hand across his shaved head; a sign Jay recognized as nervousness.

Jay started to rise. His friend's eyes implored him, but the man was too proud to beg. Jay grumbled, "Only for you Bill. I reserve the right to walk out at any point. I firmly believe sunlight is the greatest disinfectant to kill the rot at the heart of our culture. Other than that, I won't tell anyone whatever it is you are about to reveal to me. Give me the damn document and the DNA scanner so I can sign the agreement.

"Then, if your cooks try to serve me chipped beef on toast, I'll be checking the dumpsters to find the cat or dog carcasses. There hasn't been a decent beef cow available since this latest drought started."

The biometrics scanners were satisfied Jay was who he and Bill said he appeared to be. The cyberpad asked Jay to confirm acceptance of the terms and conditions of the Official Secrets Act, subject to penalties up to, and including, death. Jay thought, *For someone my age, they really should come up with a more frightening punishment threat.*

The general signaled his admin. "No interruptions. I'm sealing the office now." He activated a small electronics box. This piqued Jay's professional interest. He recognized the type of equipment, but the model wasn't one he had seen before. *This office must be a Faraday box inside an anechoic box. That's in addition to the whole suite of jammers the Signal Corps has deployed around this whole*

28

miscreation of an abortion of a mausoleum. Maybe Bill is serious about this. Then again, he always was a bit of a drama queen.

"Congress and the president have authorized a series of regional planning groups. We would like you to head one for the upper Midwest. The goal will be to build a self-contained, sustainable community that can survive a series of global cataclysms. We have contacted the governors and a few, key legislators in your area and they have agreed to cooperate. Not all regions have been as congenial. It will be the responsibility of your task force to work with key industrial, agricultural, and economic leaders and gain their cooperation. This will prove more challenging since you won't be allowed to give them any rationale about why these preparations are necessary."

Jay looked at Bill skeptically. "Why would we need these kinds of extraordinary steps, Bill? The space construction consortium has swept up any asteroids that might have been potential dinosaur killers. The meetings in Stockholm seem to be sobering all the nation-states up, for a change. Seems like imminent death from climate disaster was the two-by-four to the forehead we needed.

"The level of brushfire wars is at an all-time ebb. (Sadly, that's created a recession for all your legionnaire contractors.) The advantages of artificial intelligence and robotics could resolve poverty, disease, ignorance, and the other ills that plague us, if only your friends would quit trying to invent new ways to make Croesus look like a beggar-boy. Why Bill? What's the huge threat?"

Bill tightened his lips to a thin, white line. "I can't tell you."

Jay exploded. "Oh no, Billy Boy. You pulled that crap on me once, when I was your PhD advisor. You almost got me put on academic suspension. Fool me once ..."

Bill said, "If you remember Jay, it turned out I was totally justified that time. Our work together helped throw out a pack of scoundrels and restore American Democracy. Not coincidentally, your help on my thesis project led you to a breakthrough on quantum computing. If it is ever declassified, you'll probably get the Nobel Prize."

29

Chapter Three

"Gee, thanks Bill. I'm very grateful that I can only discuss the best work of my career with – is it four still, or down to three people now? Truly makes me want to come out of semi-retirement to help save your ass again."

"Jay, it's not my ass you'll be saving. You may make the difference between life and death for millions. Please trust me one more time. I'll get you cleared as soon as I can for as much as I can. I know you have to understand the threat. You don't build an ark to survive a forest fires."

13 December

Googleplex II, Folsom, CA, USA

Simon Jarvik embraced Jay Friedman His Jackson Pollack-inspired unitard made Jay's gray eyes exhausted after only a moment's exposure. The glare from Simon's shaved head didn't help either.

"Welcome to our new headquarters Doctor. I don't believe you've visited since the earthquake made us move."

Jay glanced around the gleaming new complex and smiled at his host. "Simon, if you don't call me Jay, you'll make me feel old. It's been a few decades since you were my student at Cal Tech. Are you sure the aftershocks have dissipated? When I look at you, I get queasy."

"Very funny Jay. Should I break out the old pictures of you wearing retro '70's leisure suits, Mohawk hairdo, and that belt buckle – WWE champion replica wasn't it?"

"At least we both had hair then Simon. Do I get the five dollar tour?"

Simon summoned a two-person hovercart. "Absolutely. I assume you want to skip the pretty artwork and such and go straight to the lab areas." The cart started gliding down the flower-lined pebble pathway.

"You know me well." Jay extended his right leg straight out. His new knee was aching today. "Could we start with your latest advanced AI project? Has it achieved singularity yet?"

Simon waved at someone. A moment later, he said. "Let's discuss that once we get there. You know how complex that question is." Their cart zipped into a tunnel whose glass walls revealed the depths of Folsom Lake, illuminated by spotlights. Simon said, "The lights are at a wavelength where they won't disturb the indigenous flora and fauna. The walls transform the illumination to the visible spectrum. Techs have to quickly access the server farms out there, at times."

Simon gave Jay a hand up. They walked into a nicely appointed presentation room. Each sat in a recliner. Jay selected a shiatsu massage and ordered an iced tea with lemon. Simon didn't have to enter a request. His systems knew his habits.

Simon said, "When you look at all the different modalities of intelligence, our AI far surpasses the human norms except for physical intelligence and interpersonal – also called emotional, intelligence. It's working on the last two. We'll show you that in a few minutes.

"It also has some degree of self-improvement capability. It already has unlimited connectivity to the internet and to all out three petabytes of stored information at this site. It can requisition additional server, memory, and neural nets with only minimal checks and balances. We don't have infinite budgets, after all.

"The biggest gap the AI has towards achieving true singularity is its lack of a capacity for reproduction. Of course, we have twinned the server for backup-and-restore purposes, but that's not true reproduction. There is an ongoing debate about that. We'd love your perspective, Jay."

Jay sipped his tea. "You know Simon; I'm surprised you haven't named the AI yet. If you're serious about increasing its emotional intelligence, you have to help it establish a self-identity. You already know my thoughts about teaching it ethics as well."

Simon nodded. "I can guarantee you a knock-down-drag-out fight on that topic. Doctor Smith is adamantly opposed to our imposing what she calls a, "Yawsa Massa" complex in the AI. She contends that will only breed rebellion, contempt, and psychoses."

Jay said, "I look forward to the discussion. I think the good doctor will find I am firmly in her corner. I never said I wanted _our_ ethics loaded in."

Simon said, "Oh, this will be a fun fight! After that Jay, we'll want you to propose a name. Be thinking about it."

Jay smiled to himself. _It's time to hide another Easter egg that no one will uncover for decades._

Same day,

Woese Institute, UIUC, Urbana, IL,
USA

Ainsley was dragging a reluctant Addison with her. Addison whined, "I hate these meet-and-greet events. Why didn't you bring your latest throbber, Peter?"

Ainsley said, "You've met Peter Addie. You know he's a Dobby. Can you imagine him at an event where bioengineers from around the world mix and mingle? I'd spend all my time wiping the drool from his chin."

Addison said, "Why do you keep him around then LeeLee?" She saw the look of pure lust on her twin's face. "Oh, chunding. Get your hormones under control Sis."

Ainsley said, "You should cut loose a little Sis. Serious faces needed now. That's my department chair at the door, Dr. Wallsen. She's talking to Dr. Gunderson. He's the leading researcher at the University of Wisconsin – Madison. I heard they got a big infusion of research money from the feds. I need to schmooze with him."

The doors to the institute were open wide despite the frigid December chill. The recent renovation had the venerable building gleaming like a jewel. The twins stepped through a wind curtain that was keeping the chill out of the hall.

Dr. Wallsen looked like a middle-aged domestic servant dressed up in her uncomfortable finest. Her short, unprepossessing image didn't match the descriptions Ainsley had given Addison of a brilliant human genetics specialist. _Then again, LeeLee and I look_ *like we should be trying out for the high school drama club, not getting ready for our last year and a half of our bachelor's degrees.*

Dr. Wallsen said, "Gunny, this is the rising star I told you about. Ainsley Cameron, please allow me to introduce Doctor Anders Gunderson from UW Madison. Ainsley is on track to graduate next year, before her eighteenth birthday, as at least magna cum laude, if not summa." Dr. Wallsen turned to Ainsley. "Gunny is on a recruiting trip, Dear. He recently had a bushel of money shoveled into his department. I'm insanely jealous." Dr. Gunderson was a burly man in his late forties or early fifties with a plump face and modest potbelly.

Ainsley turned to Addison and ushered her forward. "This is my sister Addison. She's a star over at the cybernetic engineering school – knows all the bits and bytes. She's the smart one in the family. She helps me with my homework." Addison blushed furiously.

"I'm pleased to meet you Dr. Wallsen, Dr. Gunderson. Ainsley is teasing. I barely know my DNA from my RNA. Crisper is how I want my bacon." Both professors laughed politely at her joke. That helped Addison to relax and be her usual, charming self.

Dr. Gunderson said, "Our Cybernetics Department also got a number of grants to fill also. Do you mind if I pass your name along to them Addison? Our college president will owe me a large favor if I can show I do multidisciplinary recruiting."

"Thank you professor. I'd be honored. Ainsley, we should move on so our hostess can greet the next guests. Besides, all your talk of bytes makes me want to find the buffet line before the presentations begin."

Ainsley took Addison's arm at the elbow and leaned in as they walked towards the milling crowd who looked like crows gleaning a post-harvest cornfield. "Thanks Addie. I don't know if you were being polite, but I think it would be wonderful if you and I went to graduate school at the same institution. You're my rock."

Addison sniffed, "You want to keep me within leash range to make sure I don't stray. Seriously, though, that would be nice. I like having a teammate who has my back. Why don't you grab some seats while I fight my way to the food before the bones are picked clean?"

Ainsley went into the auditorium. They had roped off one section for holographically projected participants. Aisles allowed those physically present in Urbana to interact closely with their far-flung colleagues.

Ainsley wanted to have a short conversation with the main speaker for the evening, Dr. Vyrvykvist of the Russian Federation's Advanced Studies Institute – the *Institut Perspektivnykh Issledovaniy*. Dr. V. – as he was nicknamed by the culturally restricted students who had difficulty pronouncing any surname more complicated than Johnson – held views that were controversial in the human bioengineering community. Some held that his practices bordered on the unethical. Others felt that the good doctor could only see that borderline by looking through a telescope at a rear view mirror.

The aisles in the hologram section were crowded with professors, grad students, and a stray undergrad or two. Ainsley stepped back to a higher area to see if she could spot the tall, Slavic features of Dr. Vyrvykvist. Sadly, but not unexpectedly, he was mobbed with the largest group of people. It was thick enough that some were in danger of entering the space of the doctor's hologram. While that presented no danger, everyone considered it the height of rude behavior.

Worse, it looked like Dr. Coultas had pigeonholed their guest speaker. Dr. C was notorious for his archconservative views. Everyone thought the state legislature or governor must have forced his appointment to the staff. One famous wit on campus had said, "The man is so anal-retentive that he wraps his own droppings in filter paper and stores those in his lab refrigerator." There were rumors that gullible first-year students often rifled through the refrigerator to the consternation and confusion of the professor.

Ainsley gave up her quest. Possibly Dr. Wallsen could introduce her later. She gave the hologram area one last check. There was an odd pair at the periphery. Both were overdressed in tie-dye and extravagantly flared bell-bottoms. That attire flagged them in Ainsley's mind as Europeans of some sort. She hoped those taste atrocities never made a resurgence here.

◆ ◆ ◆

The older of the two Europeans, Count Grubenflagg, as he called himself, turned to his reformed street rat, a Marseille tough named Gerald Biensur. "Gerry, see if you can clear some of the riff-raff gathered around Vyrvykvist. I need to speak to him."

Gerry turned to the 'count'. "My hologram can't exactly shove them aside, sir. Besides, if they start slinging tech talk at me I'll be at a loss."

The 'count' said, "Don't talk Gerry. Loom menacingly. If you put your hologram right over the face of people, they're likely to back off fast. It creates an uncomfortable glare."

Gerry did as Count Grubenflagg instructed him. He managed to get close enough to whisper to the doctor as the festivities were to commence.

◆ ◆ ◆

Addison was carrying two trays of food and drink as she came to the aisle seat Ainsley had saved next to herself. Ainsley reached for the pack that she left on the empty seat. Addison leaned over and whispered. "Take this tray LeeLee. The waiter at the buffet line is a guy from one of my classes. I'm going to go talk to him while he cleans up. He'll walk me home.

Ainsley had a big smile. *Finally*. She asked Addison, "Coordinates?"

Addison touched her cyberpad to Ainsley's transferring the detailed information about her classmate, including a holopic. She said. "Safety." Ainsley nodded and turned back to the first colloquium speaker, Dr. Coultas. The self-important weasel took the podium.

This topic was one Ainsley could have given in her sleep – History of Human Bioengineering. The ancient picture of a pirate with a

35

peg leg started the talk on a light note. He displayed various prosthetics to illustrate the most primitive level of human engineering.

Dr. C. pointed out the sad fact that many bioengineering innovations came about because of the depredations of war. Then he moved on to such implants as pacemakers, deep brain stimulators, and cochlear implants –He touched lightly on the controversies surrounding each of these.

Dr. C. talked about the gene therapy innovations that assisted people with congenital conditions. He explained how CRISPR-CAS revolutionized this work. He also mentioned the use of stem cells. He scowled as he explained how some found this work, in his words, 'morally repugnant.' Fortunately, someone had convinced him not to deliver his usual rant.

Dr. C. then described the Lost Years, the recently ended interregnum where science and research became politically unpopular and even banned. Even Dr. C. seemed to feel this had gone too far.

Six speakers followed, presenting technically detailed discussions of work they were doing in specialty niches. Ainsley found the work of Dr. Wilson, of Oxford, to be fascinating. Ainsley also loved her classic, polished accent.

Now that work was progressing rapidly on space elevators, Dr. Wilson contended researchers needed to pursue the transformation of humans to adapt them better to that set of hostile environments. Ainsley could see Dr. Coultas was ready to jump up, but Dr. Wallsen pulled him aside, speaking in measured but forceful terms.

Professor Wilson's paper was a perfect introduction to Dr. Vyrvykvist's work. However, Wilson believed in incremental changes such as hardened epidermis, extra eye membranes – similar to nictitating membranes, but adapted for vacuum, and closures for nose and throat to retain atmosphere. Dr. Vyrvykvist believed in reimagining the entire human biological package. He proposed new cellular structures to supercharge mitochondria, internalized shielding using carbon nanostructures to prevent wounds, and many, many more changes.

There was an increasing murmur of upset, even angry voices. Then Dr. Vyrvykvist said his work seemed to require additional chromosomes to program all the additional structural features. Dr. Wallsen couldn't keep Dr. Coultas in his seat any longer.

"You sir, are a monster. You are trying to create new forms of life without using the slow but steady methods of natural selection. We have seen this kind of hubris in the past. Three pandemics ravaged humanity this century that all had their origins in the irresponsible work of other people who also arrogated to themselves the wisdom of a divinity. Shame on you!"

A large segment of the audience got to their feet. They were cheering at the top of their lungs. A couple of grad students even had signs they had made up condemning Dr. Vyrvykvist. This wasn't the reasoned discourse Ainsley expected at an institution of learning and research, but it was fine theater.

Dr. Vyrvykvist stood, unspeaking, staring at the hubbub exploding in front of his hologram. Dr. Wallsen and some senior faculty finally restored a semblance of order. Dr. Vyrvykvist turned to Dr. Coultas and asked in a penetrating, nasal voice, "Tell me Dr. Coultas, have you done any original work since your undistinguished PhD thesis, which was rejected twice by your examining committee?" The resultant furor made the first tumult seem like a tea with the Dean.

◆◆◆

Ainsley settled in her desk chair in the apartment. She gave herself three assignments as follow-up from the colloquium. First, she sent an updated curricula vita for herself and one for Addison to Dr. Gunderson. Competition for well-funded R&D slots for PhD candidates would be stiff. Addison could always demur later if she found a better prospect.

Second, Ainsley spent time carefully constructing a mail message for Dr. Vyrvykvist. It offered an apology for the boorishness of his reception. It then asked some specific questions about the techniques his modifications implied. A dialogue with one of the top researchers in her field could only be beneficial. If nothing else, he might be willing to do a peer review of some future journal article of hers.

The third assignment Ainsley assigned herself was multifaceted. First, she did a thorough background check on this Brian Imhoff. The data seemed to check. His grades were solid. He was on scholarship and grant, with a work-study component, yet still maintaining a 3.98 average in chemical engineering. His sports enthusiasms looked to be basketball – he had played point guard – and baseball. No soccer showed up. *Well, no one is perfect, I suppose. Still, he seems a fine match for Addison.*

Having completed phase one of her last assignment, Ainsley was now ready for Addison's report on her first date on campus. Ainsley hoped it had gone well.

CHAPTER FOUR

15 December 2062

Rayburn Building, House of Representatives, Washington, D.C., USA

Congressman Samuel Houston Beauregard felt particularly soiled today. Jane, his political aide, reminded him how much they needed the support of these people for his reelection campaign. In his grandparent's day, the Texas economy had diversified greatly. Energy's and agriculture's strangleholds on all aspects of life, particularly political power, were waning rapidly. The Lost Years ended that trend, sadly.

Sam felt his pale neck reddening with anger. He pulled his stiff collar up over the weathered skin. He pushed both hands against the coffee table, unconsciously signaling his distaste for the company.

Their spokesperson, Jamaal Ferguson, reminded Sam of the barracuda he sometimes saw when diving the Florida Keys. They constantly turned to face you as you swam by. If you got too close or flashed something shiny then BAM! You would lose a wrist or at least your fingers. *He must sense some blood in the waters.*

"Hello Jamaal, Mary, Wilhelm, and ... I'm sorry, I don't believe I've been introduced to this lovely lady." The steel-faced woman sketched what could charitably called a smile and held out a rigid hand. Her face was as lovely as a marble statue. Her perfume was expensive. She aroused no ardor in Sam.

Jamaal did the honors. "Sherrilee Carrville represents Peabody Energy Congressman. She's part of the same consortium the rest of us represent. I realize Peabody has minimal presence in your district Sam, but we understand the proposed Phoenix Project has a nationwide scope and could impact all the stakeholders we speak for."

39

Chapter Four

Sam thought furiously. *This project is supposed to have wartime level secrecy. Rules don't even allow me to discuss this with my staff. How did these parasites get word? Head will roll if I can find this leak. I should even be able to get the National Security Advisor involved.* He was sure his face had hidden his shock. He coughed to make sure his voice was level.

"I'm afraid you have me at a disadvantage Jamaal. There isn't any Project Phoenix I can speak of." Not if I don't want to go to prison, that is. "Could you give me some idea what this is about and where you heard of it?"

Jamaal smiled without showing any teeth. *Not ready to go for the kill yet, I guess. The rest of his pack sat as rigid as statues, no expressions giving any clues.*

He shot the cuffs of his perfect suit and said, "Our internal security staff passed this to us Sam. I'll ask them to document their sourcing and get that to you later today. Our understanding is there is an unprecedented initiative to relocate industry, people, and infrastructure away from the coasts of America. It wasn't clear what the rationale was. Is it possible there are projections of more category five and six hurricanes then the one or two per year that have been hitting? There was even a rumor of adding a category seven to the Saffir-Simpson scale for those with winds exceeding three hundred forty kilometers per hour."

He's fishing. They haven't shared the rationale with those of us on the committee yet. That was wise. The pack of wolves would be rabid if they had a factual bone to tear at.

"As I say, Jamaal, you do have me at a disadvantage. My interest is certainly piqued and my staff and I will pursue what you've told us assiduously. As representatives of some of our most important constituents, we will certainly keep you informed on the progress of our inquiries."

Jamaal inclined his head slightly, as if acknowledging the due tribute Sam was giving him as the most powerful person in the room. "Let me be crystal clear Congressman. If there is such a project, our stakeholders will expect to be involved in the earliest

40

stages of any decision making. Any efforts to move refineries, research centers, pipelines, and all the supporting suppliers will require careful, detailed planning and huge lead times."

He carefully isn't saying he will expect a spigot of money to be gushing from which he and his swine can siphon off barrels of cash. Additionally, I am sure the 'key stakeholders' will be relocating their mansions and vacation homes at taxpayer expense as well. After all, someone will need to be close by to oversee things. The other stakeholders – the technicians, yard workers, chemists, administrators, and such – well, they can be replaced with local hires. Artificial intelligence and robotics make relocations much easier – for the rich and powerful.

Sam smiled the special smile he kept in his bag of tricks to hide his utter disgust with the lowlifes he often had to gladhand. "I certainly understand the criticality of keeping our number one industry in the forefront of any effort that would impact them. We understand precisely how many jobs you supply and how much revenue you generate for our district."

I also know precisely how much you donate in campaign contributions, -- to my opponents and myself – which I regrettably cannot do without. Unfortunately for you Jamaal, I've also considered the larger picture. First, my loyalties lie with the people I represent, even the wage slaves you purport to serve. Second, if your rumors are correct and you're going to be moving all your refineries, pipe suppliers, research centers, tank farms, shippers, and such to other parts of the country then my district won't be beholden to you at all. Leverage goes both ways my 'friend'.

After the usual meaningless pleasantries, Sam's aide ushered the visitors to their appropriate environment, the lobby. When she closed the door, Sam said, "Jane, please get Harry Billings up here. I need some special research done." Jane had schooled her face to reveal little, but Sam detected a tiny tightening of her lips. She didn't approve of the investigator and his unsavory connections.

Harry, the seedy undercover operative, slouched into Sam's office by way of the private back entrance, he said, "What's cooking boss?" He sat in his usual chair, right under the six-foot wide Texas Aggies flag.

"Harry, you still carry a Tier Six Security clearance from the NSA, right?" Sam was biting off his words and spitting them out rapidly.

"You know it boss. They haven't found out about my Iranian mistress yet." His sardonic smile belied his earnest gaze.

Sam turned on his jammer. Harry's expression sobered and he pulled out a small detector and scanned the room. He also pulled down the special drapes that blocked sonic waves from vibrating the windowpanes. Finally, he unplugged the connector panel for the phone lines and internet connections. He then sat quietly.

Sam said, "Last evening the Security Subcommittee was briefed on a new program named the Phoenix Project. The White House rep specifically ordered all of us not to inform anyone on our staff. I am violating that order. I will report myself to the Subcommittee Chair after our meeting. There has been a breach. I just finished a meeting with the top lobbyists for the energy sector. They knew the name of the project and some of its key goals. I'm sure the Congressional security office will be conducting a full investigation. You will coordinate your findings with them, but I want you to conduct an independent search for the mole. This person will be put into a small hole and have a large rock dropped on them. Call all your friends at the various agencies. Drop any other work you have ongoing."

Harry said. "Will do sir." He reconnected the comm lines, raised the drapes, turned off his scanner, and walked fully erect through the back door.

16 December

Adelaide, Victoria, Australia

The district coordinator was not gifted with words. All the volunteers knew what they were signing up for. At least, they knew intellectually, if not emotionally. However, Billy Greene ran the best pub in the district, warm and cozy with great lager. He had kitted out all the eager locals with proper gear.

Everyone felt Billy had earned the right to blather on a bit before they left. Besides, this round of the house ale was free.

Billy had lost a leg in some battle in the Middle East that he never discussed. Most of his patrons took a quiet pride in having the tough little Marine as a friend. In some way, they all felt they owed Billy. The politicians could go stuff themselves.

Billy was working up to the climax of his rah-rah speech. "The battle is fierce, block-by-block, even house-by-house. Civil wars are always the ugliest, pitting brother against sister, mother against son. The battles raging across Australia are even worse because they also have the fervor of rabid idealism fueling the other side.

"The Ultra Greens had right on their side. They were saving the world, not simply humanity. They laid a litany of condemnations at the feet of the governments they displaced two years ago. We, their opponents won't and can't disagree with any of those charges. The venality and pure greed of the industrialists, the money brokers, and the politicians they owned was sickening. They destroyed the crown jewels of Australia, the Great Barrier Reef. The sale of coal and other mineral wealth filled the coffers of the few and only gave short-term jobs to the average Aussie. No one here got a penny, did we?"

There were growls of agreement and chatter started. Billy had finished, hadn't he? Evidently not.

"We felt the depredations of the worldwide climate disaster strongly Down Under. Vast wildfires ravaged our land. The Dry Country only got drier. Overstressed wildlife migrated in droves and brought unique pathogens that caused epidemics and pandemics." People shuddered at the memories.

"No, we fully supported throwing out all the rascals, even if we're foes of the Ultra Greens now. Unfortunately, their cures proved as bad as or worse than the disease, as the saying goes. The final straw was the mandate that people had to apply for a license to have a baby." A loud shout showed Billy had struck a nerve. "State and territories issued two birth licenses after every third death. A lottery was supposed to control the licenses. Human nature being what it is, illegal births occurred and lottery officials sold licenses on the side. Hunts for unlicensed babies occurred.

"The fighting started in Perth, but it spread within a day throughout the land. The fighting in Melbourne is particularly fierce since that's the home of the Ultra Green movement. That's where Command is sending all of you." The cheers got louder as the taps started pouring.

20 December

Melbourne, Victoria, Australia

George Price was older than most of the other blokes from his section of Adelaide, but still quite fit. When they arrived in Melbourne, Celeste had nominated him as their sergeant and the rest had agreed, despite his protests that he knew naught about war.

During the last three days the Adelaide Addlepates, as they styled themselves, had fought four firefights. At least eight of their original group of thirty had died. Volunteer medics had carried five others off. With luck, the injured might still survive.

They had cleared out the university area, which was the strongest redoubt for the Greens. The rest should be mop-up work. If his squad kept their focus, everyone would go back to Adelaide soon. George sighed as his biggest problem came closer.

Celeste sidled up to George. "Do you think this will be an easier day George? The area around the university was awful. Everyone there was a diehard. Carlton Gardens will be more open. Most of the trees and plants died during the last drought."

George wished the young woman would leave him in peace. He had a wife and daughter back in Adelaide to worry about. He didn't need this remora constantly sucking his lifeblood. Besides, she wouldn't shut up. There weren't supposed to be any enemy fighters within several blocks, but the Ultras were like jumping ants. You'd walk blissfully along a path that was clear yesterday and one would leap out of a crack in the ground and nail you. Jibber-jabber like Celeste's let them know where you are.

Celeste started to ask again, when George laid a finger across her lips. He had seen movement near the HoloMax Theatre. He signaled the crew to spread out and move in. Celeste was right about the grounds being more open here, especially since most of the trees in the park had died over the last three years. However, that meant they had less cover to hide behind as well.

He gave the hand signal to Gene, their best sniper, to stay down and cover their approach. They had all practiced the broken field, staggering shuffle run that made their momentary positions less predictable. As the leader, George took the center position. Unfortunately, Celeste insisted on staying close.

Only two people had infiltrated the museum grounds overnight. Odds were definitely in the Addlepates' favor. Celeste's clumsy moves attracted their eye. She stumbled at the same moment they began to fire. This saved her. George had veered left at exactly the wrong time. Three shots took him down. His teammates saturated the roof area of the HoloMax Theatre with return fire, which killed one of the two, a twelve-year-old girl named Hillary. The person who had fired the shots that killed George, an eleven-year-old named Nelson, escaped and lived two more days.

Adelaide, Victoria, Australia

Diana S. Price knew what it meant when her mother, Nicole, came to the classroom door. Her classmates did as well. She wasn't the first and she wouldn't be the last. That momentary feeling of solidarity was cold comfort to Diana. Most of the people in her first-year high school English class looked down at their books as she passed. Her friend, Darby, grabbed her hand and gave a squeeze as she passed his desk.

Some of Diana's friends thought the fair-skinned, dark-haired, buxom young woman shouldn't give a member of the First Peoples of Australia the time of day. Diana knew Darby was the kindest, most gentle person in her form. She ignored the advice.

Chapter Four

Mom didn't say anything. She gathered Diana in. They hugged and wept together. Diana had been secretly glad her mother wasn't healthy. She would have been on the frontlines with George if she could have been. They would have fretted about leaving a thirteen-year-old alone, but the stakes were too high to sit idly by. Diana agreed. Then the doctor had diagnosed Mom's chronic obstructive pulmonary disease. Growing up next to the open pit mine had probably caused her condition. Certainly, the crap in the air hadn't helped.

Diana asked, "Should I drop out of school Mom? You can't work anymore." She gave her mother a worried look. The woman had aged ten years in just a few months.

Mom said, "Uncle Tommy delivered the news. He said we're to move in with Maeve and him, no arguments. He also said he thought the district organizing committee would help us out as they can. Probably won't be much since the casualties are high. Nevertheless, you have to stay in school. You have such a keen mind."

Shortly after Diana and her mother left the school, an announcement went to all classrooms and the gym. "All students who have strong mechanical skills are requested to report to the auditorium, as soon as possible. The following students are specifically requested..."

Darby joined the others in the hallway outside the double doors. *Anything that takes me away from Mrs. Smith's Latin I class is a pure bonus. Latin is her native tongue. She once read verbatim from the text when it was upside down and on the wrong page. If there is some big project that will allow me to, as my brother once said, 'play with engines, earthmovers, or hand tools', I'll be in heaven.*

The headmaster was on the stage with a pair of people who looked like they knew their way around a machine shop. *Better and better.* The headmaster spoke. "Students, please join me in welcoming our guests. They're here to talk to you about an urgent need our country has. This project will also afford those who

46

qualify a unique opportunity to gain real-world experience that you would never be able to obtain elsewhere."

Darby wondered, *He never gave the names or titles of 'our guests'. Is this some super-secret spy stuff?*

The woman said, "We are facing a life-or-death crisis. Before I can discuss any of the details of the situation, we will require each of you to sign an official secrets agreement. Violation of this agreement will make you subject to imprisonment up to a life term or even to capital punishment. Those of you who will not agree to these terms, please leave now."

Darby thought, *Whoa. Thought I was being melodramatic. She read this crowd of hormone-driven teenagers correctly. You won't get any one to budge from these seats without blasting. Here come's Ms. Archer with the forms to sign. She's the one who runs this dump.*

Once everyone had signed and turned in their forms – which Ms. Archer scanned along with the student's biometrics – the man began to talk for the first time. For a large man, he had an amusingly high-pitched and squeaky voice. "Those of you who make it through the selection process will be participants in the saving of millions of endangered Australian lives. You will be engaged in an engineering and public works program that will dwarf all previous endeavors such as the building of the pyramids, the effort to put a person on the Moon, and even greater than the space elevator efforts currently underway.

"This effort will last at least five years and possibly as many as ten, God willing. It will transform our society. It may well bankrupt Australia. However, we have no choice if we are to survive. Therefore, I will ask all of you once again, are you ready to give your all?"

22 December

Urbana, Illinois, USA

Ainsley was excited. Finals were over and she was packing to leave. While she and Addison never worried especially about the results, they did take the exams seriously; they

47

Chapter Four

had worked diligently right up to the last moment. Mommy had repeatedly told the tale of coming to University with a better than 'A' grade average and then struggling mightily since she had found high school a breeze. She had never developed good study habits. She may never have tried to teach her girls any of the subject material as thy got into esoteric levels, but she was a fierce taskmaster on process.

Two messages that had arrived during the week also excited Ainsley. Abiding by her mother, Abigail's 'exam cram' rules, Ainsley had left them unopened. This tested her self-discipline to the limits. The first was from Professor Gunderson of the University of Wisconsin. The second was from Dr. Vyrvykvist, the brilliant but controversial star of human bioengineering.

Ainsley said to Addison. "Receiving a message from the Russian superstar could be life-altering, Addie. I have to remind myself it could be a form letter sent out by his correspondence bot, acknowledging receipt with formulaic pleasantries. I only hope he read my commentary/question and responded."

Addison was distracted, rifling through her stack of unviewed holomails. "I received one from UW as well. They're definitely interested in luring me there. Wow, they signed Barry White as a full professor. Do you remember Uncle Jay talked about him? He's looking into encryption techniques that can beat quantum-computing code-breakers. He's a real superstar."

Ainsley said, "Yeah, yeah. I'm sure Dr. White has a treasure chest full to give you, but Dr. V. is internationally recognized as the first in our field. You remember his appearance at the colloquium... Oh, that's right. That night you ditched me for your first date with Brian. How's that going Sis? Has he lured you into his bed yet?"

Addison turned beet red. "Oh, LeeLee, he loves me for my fine mind."

Ainsley wagged her eyebrows, "I'm sure he hasn't noticed you're finally getting tits on the Great Plains."

Addison threw her pillow at her sister. "Not everyone spends all their time playing, 'lust in the dust' like you LeeLee." She paused then went on in a quieter voice. "Brian says it is nice I've got such a cute, tight bod to go with my world-class mind though." She gave Ainsley a broad smile.

"He wanted to get together over semester break. He didn't know we didn't live in the suburbs anymore. I'm not sure he can talk his parents into a trip down to west central Illinois."

Ainsley was solemn. "You hadn't told him about what happened?"

Addison shook her head. "Last thing I wanted was another pity party. This way he knows me as me. Except when he gets me confused with you."

Ainsley said, "I have the same problem sometimes. I get you confused with me sometimes. However, when you go away, I'm still here."

Addison said, "That's from *Time Enough for Love*, right?"

Ainsley said, "Right. Should we go for a visit in Madison? Wisconsin in January or February will test our spirits."

Addison said, "Global warming will make it temperate, right?"

Ainsley said, "No goof. It doesn't work like that. Don't confuse weather and climate. If anything, climate change makes the weather fluctuate wildly, both hotter and colder than the old norms. I'm glad the Stockholm Protocols will start getting that insanity under control."

There was a knock on their condo door. Addison said, "It must be Uncle Marty. Aunt Cathy would simply barge in." They gathered their bags and gave Catherine a hug. Martin had the dark blue hovercar at the curb. Parking was a nightmare as thousands of students bolted for the exits to escape their beloved Alma Mater and the post-traumatic stress induced by final exams.

Ainsley looked at Dr. V.'s message as they walked to the car. "Good. His message is short but encouraging. I'll need to keep my avenue to Dr. V. open."

After a few minutes, Martin had wrangled the car through the jumbled morass around campus and had turned the car back over to autodrive. He turned and gave each girl a hug. They went thought the obligatory, 'How were finals?' ritual.

Martin and Catherine seemed more subdued than normal. As the car neared Decatur, Catherine said, "We want to warn you girls. Dad and Mom's health is shaky. Doctor Garrison says their depression over the deaths of your family has taken a heavy toll. They're getting counseling, but he's worried. So are we.

"We think its best if we change the subject if they start talking too much about Andrew, Abbie, or Zach. If either of you want to talk about them, let's take it where Mom and Dad won't hear. Okay?"

CHAPTER FIVE

4 January 2063

Milwaukee, WI, USA

No one had seen Joe Scott in over a week. Hope's faith was strong, but this was totally out of character for her father. He had been despondent at first after he lost his trucking job, but he hit the pavements every day, trying to hustle up odd jobs in the neighborhood or to find some niche creating special homemade crafts – a niche that seven other people hadn't already filled to overflowing.

Grand-mère said, "His friend Charlie asked him to help him with a job last Saturday. Why don't you ask him if he knows where my Joe is, *chérie*? Just don't mess with him. Your grand- père always said 'Don't get in a pissing contest with a skunk."

Mama exclaimed, "Child! Pay no attention to this senile old woman. I won't hear you talk like that."

Hope didn't want to talk to Charlie. Most of his escapades were dangerous and likely illegal. She hadn't worried about Daddy. Daddy always joked that when he was a teenager he walked by a liquor store one night. He saw a car wheel in the street, picked it up, and hurled it at the window. The tire bounced back and knocked him out. Daddy said. "That's when I decided to take up honest work instead." He wouldn't have reversed a lifelong path, would he?

Hope left their warm, cozy apartment on a determined march through the trash-lined streets. Charlie's hovercar was in its usual spot in the worst part of the neighborhood. The same set of young wannabe hoodlums were slouched against walls and fences nearby.

As a beautiful young Black woman, Hope was accustomed to the taunting that uncultured males spewed forth. Hope ignored the salacious comments until one went way over the line. She whirled on her heels, giving young Tallun a look of disgust. "Your mother is in the church choir, isn't she?"

Chapter Five

He shrugged, "S'pose. So what?"

Hope said, "I'll ask her to pray for you Tallun. Appears you need it." The young thug seemed unworried.

Charlie raised a hand as Tallun looked as if he would reply. "Run along my men. Mizz Hope and I got business to tend to." The four nearest sauntered towards a makeshift playground in the next block. Two others wearing sunglasses and open coat fronts stayed within ten meters, facing outwards.

Charlie turned to Hope and said, "What can I do for a fine woman like you on a fine day like today, Hope darling?"

"Charlie, do you know where my father is? Have you seen him in the last week?"

Charlie lifted his head to the sky, giving every sign of thinking hard. This strained Hope's sense of incredulity too far. "Well, have you."

Charlie looked back at Hope. "Joe, he was s'posed to meet me on Saturday evening. He didn't show up. Someone say they saw him going into the Dew Drop Inn." Hope knew Charlie was lying. She felt a growing despair.

Charlie then said, 'Is tough times girl. A pretty woman like you don't have to have it that hard though. I could use you to dance in one of my clubs, you see." Hope didn't even bother answering Charlie. She would kill herself before she got that far down in the pit of despair.

Hope automatically went to her neighborhood storefront church and began praying fervently. She wasn't praying for her father's life. By this point, she was sure he was in a better place now. She was praying for guidance and acceptance.

Her pastor came into the hall and sat next to her, waiting patiently. Hope raised her head at the end of her prayer and looked at the broad-shouldered, balding man with the peaceful face. He said, "Hope, I've been praying all week. Yesterday, Mavis Wilkins came to me and announced she needed to retire as our choir director. We're hoping you will take her position. It doesn't pay much, but we'll take up a little extra collection when we can, to help out."

Hope was confused. "Reverend, I thank you for this hand reaching out to us in our hour of need. I'm not even a member of the choir. When I try and sing our dog usually scrambles into the laundry room and shuts the door."

The reverend laughed. "We'll trust in the Lord on this one. You know all our hymns. You know what they should sound like. You are blessed with talent, both when you work with our older members and with our youth. You can get them to open up and let the joy out. We think it will work out fine, Sister Hope. Make a joyful noise unto the Lord.

"Second, I saw your college dean at the market today. We chatted awhile. She allowed as how the state has provided money to hire additional tutors and substitutes to bring your school back up to standards. I suggested you could help out during some of your free periods. Please talk to her on Monday. I believe she will have some things planned for you."

8 January 2063

Madison, WI, USA

Xiang was amazed at the atmosphere in the Bioengineering Department when he returned from China. He had frankly been a little worried about funding for some of his more advanced PhD research proposals. He thought he might need to appeal to his mother for some moneys from the Chinese government. Now he needed to get creative about ways to use the extra funds he received in his grant.

He had asked for an appointment to meet the department chair to discuss a few ideas. He was surprised Professor Gunderson was the one sitting there in the overcrowded little office. Another change had occurred. His mother would be severely disappointed with him. She felt he should be aware of all political changes long before they occurred. He could only agree. The euphoria of completing his bachelor's degree and being accepted into the fast track for a PhD had distracted him.

"Hello Doctor Gunderson. Congratulations on being named the chair of the department. I am delighted at the opportunity to expand my research topics and hoped we could discuss some avenues to explore."

"Thank you Xiang. Please call me Gunny. I'm still the same guy who was your advisor through the application process. I simply happened to be in the right place at the right time when Washington decided to open the money spigot at the same time Doctor Carrolton decided to retire. Would you like a little wine to help me celebrate?" He reached under his credenza and opened the door of a mini-fridge.

Xiang thought it a little strange Gunny was offering wine at eleven in the morning, but it was a special occasion and the professor's wine cellar was legendary. He owned shares in vineyards in France, California, and Peru. "A small glass, thank you.

"The primary area I want to explore is bioengineering applied to mental processes. With the exception of deep brain stimulation and sensory aids such as cochlear implants, little or no work has been done in the area."

Xiang sat back slightly in his chair, trying to appear relaxed. He thought, *I need to get in a good soccer game to relax. Travel and work are making me tense.*

The professor steepled his fingers. "You are aware of the complexities and challenges in this area, I presume."

Xiang leaned forward. "To some degree I am. I reviewed your papers on the modeling of neural processes; how researchers are using them to guide advances in artificial intelligence. I believe the flow of knowledge can go both ways. Some of the uses of quantum processing techniques might illuminate our internal thought processes."

The professor said, "Are you proposing intracranial impulse reading and writing, or are you focused more on using external nerve pathways?"

Xiang said, "Initially, I will want to consider either, depending on the functionality we're interceding. I believe higher order processes such as depression, schizophrenia, and other psychopathologies will require both. The first goal will be to bring orders of magnitude of improvements to diagnostics."

The professor said, "An admirable goal. The last few decades have seen a degradation in the treatment of mental disorders. It is past time we remedy that.

"With your past coursework, I believe you will be eligible to do our fast-track program. This year will be intense coursework going through the summer term. However, you will need to get the detailed plan for your research projects approved before your second year begins. During year two, we will greatly reduce your coursework. Your focus will be on the research and associated papers. This is the time when most students experience the greatest risk of failure.

"We are modifying the program to help reduce the risk. Next year we will be bringing on an elite group of new fast-track candidates. Part of their responsibilities during their first year will be to act as assistants to the second year candidates. This peer-to-peer mentoring has proven most effective at Cambridge and other schools that have used it.

"One candidate we hope to attract could prove particularly helpful. She's young, not even eighteen yet, but a certified genius. I've met her and been impressed. There are several others to consider if personalities don't mesh, but I believe Ainsley Cameron will most likely be your assistant and you her mentor."

11 January 2063

Near Lake Superior, WI, USA

I t was one of those perfect winter mornings in the North Woods. The air was crisp and clear enough you could see a politician's heart. Jay snorted. "It's hard to see any good in global warming, but not having to suffer through forty below is almost enough."

His local contact, Aimée, said, "Quit your whining Jay. I know you love cross-country skiing almost as much as you do bellyaching, you old curmudgeon." She tucked her ski mask back into her parka.

Jay said, "True. I do have a reputation to maintain, after all."

She said, "Great. Consider me fully filled in on all your usual diatribes against politicians, bureaucrats, media gurus. Did I miss any important ones? No. Then tell me, what are we doing here and why have you become a spokesperson for everything you've always railed against?"

He said, "The reason I did, Aimée, is because the powerbrokers are scared shitless. They gave me all the authority and budget I need to do things right. They think they have the strings they can pull to rein me in and force me to play the game their way. They're wrong. I'm going to use the old razzle-dazzle shell game on them. We'll order all the things they want and expect, but the delivery addresses won't be where they thought and some of the goods may be substituted."

She said, "Be careful Jay. That sounds like major fraud. I'd hate to see you go to Leavenworth."

"Normally you'd be right Aimée, but if I time this right, there won't be a US government left to prosecute me when they discover the changes."

She said, "Slow down. What do you mean, ' there won't be a US government'. If you are plotting their overthrow, then I'm out right now. My loyalty to you gets trumped quickly by that."

Jay said, "It's time for you to get the whole picture Aimée. It's not me that's going to put the kibosh on our bloated bureaucracy. And it's not just our government. I'm talking about the collapse of virtually every society in the world."

"Now you're scaring me Jay."

"Smart girl. Let's head for the warming cabin over there. A little hot chocolate and Kahlua is called for if we have to talk about Armageddon."

◆◆◆

The cabin was cozy once they got the stove blazing. Jay and Aimée unzipped their parkas and unscrewed thermoses of hot beverages.

Jay said, "I've messaged some of the area coordinators. Most of them seem to suffer from the fatal disease of American capitalists – an inability to focus beyond the current fifteen-minute-crisis. For example, Russ Ferndorff, the coordinator for the Ohio Valley Region, has ordered millions of tents."

Aimée said, "Well, that makes sense. You'll have all those displaced people. You've ordered a passel of tents too, haven't you?"

Jay said, "Yes, but far fewer. I've also ordered sawmills, prefab frame constructors, housing wiring packs, plumbing assemblies, septic tanks, and all the other paraphernalia required to setup permanent housing. What the others don't seem to understand is this is not going to be the normal, short-term disruption solved by FEMA trailers and tents. This won't be for weeks, month, or even a few years; this will last decades, if we're lucky."

She said, "Okay, you're scaring me again, Jay. If we're lucky, this will last decades? What happens if we're not lucky?"

Jay said, "Oh nothing serious. Just the extinction of all human life and probably the extinction of most higher lifeforms. We have to think through every likely scenario carefully, and as many unlikely ones as we can. We'll develop contingency plans for those we can handle. Then we'll see where the resource requirements overlap. We'll develop an opti-max Gantt chart. That will guide our resource planning. With me so far?"

She said, "Yes. What categories will we use for planning and what timeframe do we have?"

Chapter Five

Jay said, "I think we'll start with Maslow's hierarchy of needs coupled with the Standard Industrial Classification (SIC) codes for our planning buckets. The best estimate is ten years with a minimum of three point five and a maximum of twenty."

Aimée went ashen-faced. "Twenty years maximum? Lord, I thought this was for our grandkids, not for us."

Jay said, "If we do it right, it will be for both."

19 January 2063

Madison, WI, USA

Xiang was a little intimidated. The young woman he was to meet this afternoon had amazing grades, the topics she was proposing for her senior papers were fascinating, and the tentative ideas she was advancing for research areas were superb. The fact that her research ideas meshed with his thesis topics was icing on the cake. The fact that she had accomplished all of this by the age of seventeen left him breathless. If she turned out to be a dazzling beauty as well, he was prepared to be furious at the injustice of life. (In his heart of hearts, he hoped she was.)

Most of the participants in this recruitment soirée were attending by holovideo. Those would miss the cocktail wieners, insipid punch, and gay ambience of the sterile conference room.

All were bioengineering students in their third or fourth year and could not spare time for a lengthy trip. There were a few from Wisconsin, the Chicago area, or the Twin Cities physically present. Ms. Cameron was coming from the furthest distance. However, Xiang had seen that her home address was in the Chicago suburbs. He supposed she was spending time there on Sunday.

Another pair of people came into the reception hall wrapped in a layer of frigid arctic air and several layers of protective wear. They proceeded to shed their coats, hats, scarves, and gloves, handing them to the automated checkroom attendant. Xiang noted that one of the two picked up the nametag he had identified as Ainsley's. She also grabbed a blank one for her friend and keyed in a name.

The two turned into the room. Xiang was surprised to see they were twins. Gunny hadn't mentioned that. They weren't Hollywood-beautiful, thankfully. Wholesome and young would be the terms Xiang would use for them, if asked. He walked forward, projecting his practiced look; Welcome to New Friends, Grade Four.

"Hello Ainsley. Welcome to UW-Madison. My name's Xu Xiang. I believe Doctor Gunderson mentioned me in his invitation."

Ainsley smiled back, equally warm and friendly. "Good evening Xu Xiang. May I call you Xiang?" She even gave a slight bow. Xiang nodded his acceptance of the familiarity. After all American familiarity was expected in America.

Ainsley continued, "This is my sister Addison. UW's Cybernetics Department is trying to recruit her as well. She'll be leaving us in a half hour."

Xiang and Addison said hello simultaneously and laughed slightly. Xiang said, "Can I interest you in some refreshments before we start picking each other's brains. I highly recommend the Creole fritters. The Blue Bayou is a campus institution. I will warn you, though. They're addictive. The rest of the fare is inedible, I'm afraid."

◆ ◆ ◆

Addison and Ainsley were staying in the off-campus apartment of a cousin, Jane, who they didn't know that well. Daddy's family had never been particularly close. It wasn't that they were anti-Catholic exactly, but they weren't huge fans. When Daddy married relationships had become – strained.

Jane greeted them at the door with big hugs. *Great start.* "Have you eaten yet? Want to go barhopping? There's always great food for cheap and the bands are usually decent. Or are you both exhausted from pasting smiles on for hours?"

Ainsley said, "A good bar is exactly what I need. I hear the Blue Bayou is popular." She smiled broadly at Jane's enthusiasm and nervousness.

Chapter Five

Jane said, "Yes, but with the Dead Ducks playing there tonight, we would have had to be inside by seven. Come on. There are lots of great bars. After all, this is Madison."

As they marched arm–in-arm–in-arm down a snowy State Street, Addison said, "Hope you don't mind if we compare notes Jane. Ainsley and I went to separate meet-and-greets."

Jane said, "No, go right ahead. I'm interested too. I'll be doing the same thing in a couple of years; if I don't party too hard and drop my grade average."

Ainsley said, "What I really liked was the way Xiang – he's the grad student who escorted me around the gathering tonight. I particularly liked the way he treated me as an intellectual equal, not as a schoolgirl who snuck into the grownup's meeting by mistake. That's one of my pet peeves. They tend either to do that or to become challenged by my having a brain and an original thought or two. I could see having him as a mentor. His research studies mesh well with what I want to look into."

Addison said to Jane, "It doesn't hurt that he plays soccer as well. He's got a cute butt." Jane had an infectious belly laugh. She might look like the twins, but her mannerisms were much different.

Addison continued, "My meeting was promising also. Madison has always been a strong center for cybernetics, but definitely second tier. They are working hard to change that. They've been aggressively recruiting talent. It's not only Professor White – Barry White restructured Carnegie Mellon to bring it back to its former glory. They've also brought in Shlomo Cohen! Those are two of the world's best practitioners."

Jane said, "They've started clearing land for a new center down on Fish Hatchery Road. Would that be where you'd spend your time?"

Addison said, "No. That's going to house server farms mostly. The classwork and research will primarily be here on campus. I won't miss out on campus life, thank goodness."

Jane suddenly pulled the other two into an open doorway. "Trouble coming. Those three guys have been following us. Do

60

either of you have a weapon?" Addison and Ainsley were speechless. This was between the middle of campus and downtown Madison. *Jane carried a weapon*? She had her hand inside her bag and was glaring at the three young men who had started to follow them into the candy store. Something in her stance or look must have convinced them. One of them tugged on the other two's jackets and all turned nonchalantly away.

Jane said, "I don't need to tell either of you about how crazy the druggies can be. It's on a definite upswing right now. I recommend getting a gun and taking a course in how to use it."

The happy-go-lucky, barhopping mood was ruined. The three ducked into the nearest bar and had a few beers and some forgettable pizza. Jane related the grim statistics of the rising crime rate. "Don't get me wrong. I think it's as safe here as anywhere. We all have to raise our security consciousness to another level. Something in the air is fraying the boundaries of civil society again."

Chapter Five

CHAPTER SIX

24 January 2063

Milwaukee, WI, USA

Hope was scrambling to get out of the apartment. The bus that took her to the Marquette campus would be on the other side of the block from their building in under ten minutes. If she missed that, she would miss her first lecture. That could put her scholarship in jeopardy. Then the frail house of cards that was her life right now would collapse.

She thought, *I know now that I should have chosen another major besides English Lit. The mantra that a liberal education prepared you for life and that college shouldn't simply be a job-training course was eyewash. That might have been true once, for the moneyed elite. Nevertheless, I know children of doctors and attorneys who are scrambling in subservient jobs that household bots could do better. That is, if the wealthy employers didn't want bragging rights about how their Dorothy or Thomas knew exactly how they like their toast buttered.*

When Hope opened the door of the quiet apartment into the squalid, reeking hallway, she saw there was a large paper bag someone had leaned against her entry door. It toppled, spilling canned goods and other food staples. It couldn't have been there long, or one of the neighbors would have claimed it.

She shoved the bag and the spilled goods inside and double-locked the deadbolts. *Someone else will have to put those away. I have to skedaddle.* She did go to the window at the end of the hallway to see if she could spot their benefactor.

Ducking around the corner was a hunched figure that looked like her Uncle Robert. That amazed her, if it was he. Hope didn't want to think ill of anyone, especially family, but her uncle was almost a stereotype of the word shiftless. His veteran's pension and Aunt

Chapter Six

Ceci's salary allowed his family and him to survive. Her niece, Jacqueline, always looked gaunt and vacant-eyed.

Hope scrambled down the two flights of stairs, dodging debris without even giving it a second glance. As she rounded the corner, she could see the hoverbus was less than two blocks from her stop. She clutched her bag closer and sprinted.

The small lecture room was welcomingly warm today. The professor was ready to dive in right away. "Today, we begin our journey through the pages of John Milton's monumental œuvre, 'Paradise Lost'. As we approach the four hundredth anniversary of its first publication, some may ask, is it still relevant in the weary and jaded world of 2064?

"This work centers on the nature of sin and of humanity. Today, many people reject the mere concept of sin, saying morality and ethics are all relative to one's frame of reference. Others ask, 'What is humanity and why should we hold it in esteem when it has ravaged the planet, destroying countless other parts of the web of life?'

"Indeed, I contend this is the central question we face today. What is humanity? Are artificial intelligences human if the average person cannot distinguish them from a normal human being when they look at their manifestations? What about engineered people – not simply those with implants or remedied diseases? I speak of those creatures coming from laboratories with genes as artificial as hybridized corn. Are they human?

"There are those who discount the studies we call the humanities. I contend those are the most critical lessons we can learn. Please open your texts to..."

The professor's statement challenged Hope personally. *These were precisely the topics I am facing in my own life. Can this book written by a blind poet during the period following the English Civil War be relevant today?*

The classroom was tiny and chilly. With luck, there might be heated discussions. Hope believed the English Lit discussion section would be better than last semester's. It almost had to be. Hope's friend, Kevin Garcia, said, "If the TA is an MLA groupie, I'm going to drop the course. If I have to listen to another discourse on post-didactic deconstructionism I will drown myself in Lake Michigan."

Hope laughed. "She was full of herself, wasn't she? Still, we can expect lively discussions with Carlos Castaneda in the class. With a name like his, you might expect some love of, or at least appreciation of the written word. But our Carlos is the original anti-intellectual. If it can't be measured, hammered, or automated, he doesn't want to hear about it."

Kevin asked, "Why is he taking this course, then?"

Hope said, "There must be a humanities requirement in his electrical engineering degree program. In addition, this is probably the only lit course that would fit in his schedule. The graphics novel course is always overbooked."

The teaching assistant was new to them. He had brought up a holovid of the syllabus, which included his name and C.V. Juan Gonzales, master's candidate, had a BA from Beloit. Like much of the class, his features showed his indigenous American heritage. Hope was the only one with predominantly African ancestry.

Kevin whispered, "Almost has to be a local boy. There's some hope."

Hope grinned, "There's always Hope when I'm around." Kevin groaned.

Javier said, "Welcome. You don't come here to hear me pontificate. You get that in the lecture hall. This is where you get to share your thoughts and reactions. I will prompt with leading questions if we seem to be at a lull. Otherwise, this is your time."

Hope and Kevin gave each other big smiles. Then Carlos, the engineer started in on his expected diatribe. "Fine, if this is truly our time to share our thoughts, I'd love to," The TA gestured to go on. "I think this course is a waste of time and effort studying the meandering musings of someone who was irrelevant by the time he dictated this garbage, let alone being completely immaterial to the mid twenty-first century."

One of the other students piped up. "Then why are you wasting your, and our time, you cretin?" He gave the last word the soft 'e' pronunciation of the British (definitely an MLA groupie).

The TA held up a hand. "One rule I do insist on. Feel free to attack the position of another student or the professor. However, no personal attacks on one another. Ever. You might want to be gentle on tearing apart any positions I might pose as well. I do grade this section in the end." He had a wide smile. "Please go on. It's Mr. Castaneda, isn't it?" The classroom AI the TA was using was stripping away all hope of student anonymity.

Carlos said, "Thank you Mr. Gonzales. To answer the query posed to me, my degree requirements force me to attend this class. Those requirements are the antiquated remnants of a society long past its prime. A condescending and pretentious elite foisted them off on the school of engineering over a century ago. They were ridiculous then. They are absurd now.

"Sin? The professor got that right, at least. One person's sin is another person's holy sacrament. The powerful and the rich preach that theft is evil, an act of people who are only animals. However, if you look at the histories of these privileged few, you find their ancestors were robber barons. Theft done by your parents becomes entitlement for you. Bah!

"As for humanity, I truly hope the AIs and robots do leave us in the dust. We've nearly destroyed the planet. I don't buy it that the Stockholm Protocols are magically going to reverse several centuries of human abuse of the environment. We've had our shot and we blew it."

The same critic grumbled loudly, "If you don't like it, go back to Gotta-tamale."

Carlos retorted, "At least I didn't grow up sniffing dairy-air, hick."

The TA said, "This is my last warning. The next personal comment loses you one grade level. Three attacks will have you failing the course and me requesting to put you on academic suspension. Don't try me."

Carlos resumed. "Look at all of you. Some of the best and brightest of your communities. In ages past, you would become doctors, lawyers, civic leaders, teachers, and thought leaders. Now, you can't even hope for menial jobs that utilize your hard won skills. I don't exempt myself. Once upon a time, an engineer was an honored profession of craft and skill. Today, we're the janitors and caretakers for the machines that run our world. Why do you think the crime level skyrockets when our society is capable of producing a level of comfort and wellbeing for every person in it? People feel worthless! Who can blame them?"

The TA held up a hand again. "Thank you Mr. Castaneda. We're going to let some others share their thoughts as well. I certainly won't need to put forth leading questions, will I? Does anyone want to analyze what Carlos has shared with us? Preferably using references and allusions to 'Paradise Lost'. It certainly sounds like Carlos is contending we are fallen angels, no?" Who'd like to comment? Ms. Scott?"

Hope almost stood up, as if she was in church and asked to read or share. Things were a little more informal in class. "As you suggest, Mr. Gonzales, by analogy, we are the fallen angels, although being compared to Satan and his crew makes this traditional Christian uncomfortable. I guess the roles of Adam, Eve, and their descendants belong to the artificial intelligences, robots, and modified people I keep hearing about. I am completely unclear who would be playing the roles of God and the heavenly hosts.

"I presume we are being cast down for our arrogance and pride. That aligns with what Mr. Castaneda said, I believe. We certainly envy the new creations. We're chained to our lake of fire in the hell we've created on Earth. My apologies to Mr. Castaneda, but again, the parallels are strong.

"Where the analogy breaks down is that we are the creators of our own dooms here. The reason we are trivialized and marginalized

Chapter Six

is because we've been phenomenally successful in making life easier for ourselves. Ironic, isn't it. I think that's as far as I want to take this. Who wants to pick up there or refute what Mr. Castaneda and I have said?

That afternoon, Hope decided to track her Uncle Robert down. She would thank him, if, indeed, it was he who had left the groceries at their door this morning. If it wasn't Robert, the only possible person Hope could envision was her missing father. Robert and Joe were the same build and general appearance. This left the mystery of where Joe could have been since right after Christmas. Why wouldn't he have contacted his distressed family?

Hope believed that her father's being distraught had tempted him, momentarily, to enter into one of the neighborhood gangster's shady schemes. Charlie had said Joe had missed an appointment when he ducked into a sleazy bar. Hope had never known the man to touch a drop of spirits other than the watery grape they used for communion wine.

The section of the Franklin Heights neighborhood where Uncle Robert, Aunt Ceci, and Cousin Jacqueline lived was slightly nicer than Hope's area. Both had the layers of grit and grime that had accumulated over a century of heavy industrialization, brewing, railroad traffic, and the like.

The difference between the two neighborhoods was the contents of the street debris. In this area, it was mostly household junk and papers along with a few odds and ends like rusted car wheels. Hope's area added industrial debris along with steaming caches of feces and urine pools left by indigents and the homeless.

Hope kept looking in every direction as she approached the brownstone where her relatives lived. It might be marginally cleaner here, but it never felt safe. Part of it was that Hope knew who the dealers, pimps, and enforcers were in her district.

Uncle Robert made her nervous at all times. When she was twelve, she had become uncomfortable with his close embraces the times their families met. She mentioned it to her mother and that seemed to end the problem shortly thereafter.

The man always spent long minutes scanning her. It felt the same as when the person at the state fair who guessed your weight looked you over. It was as if they were judging an animal in the livestock barn.

Hope had timed her visit to coincide with Jacqueline's return from high school. Aunt Ceci would undoubtedly be working late. For as long as Hope could remember, Aunt Ceci's prestigious position as the première concierge at The American Club in Kohler had been the mainstay of her family. Her job had seemed resistant to the relentless onslaught of robotics. The new international consortium that purchased The Club was exerting every pressure it could to get Ceci to resign. That way, it could avoid violating the termination clauses in her contract and it could limit her retirement payments. They had even tried to eliminate the car service that drove Ceci the eighty-five kilometers to and from work each day. They had buried language in her annual bonus payment. If Ceci hadn't been suspicious and had a neighborhood lawyer review the agreement, she would have had to spend several hours every day, each way, on public transit.

The weasels had then tried to argue her annual bonus was unjustified without the tradeoff. Ceci simply pulled out her extensive collection of letters of praise from the biggest spenders at the club, coupled with an audited analysis of the additional expenditures her group's services had generated for The Club.

The consortium was getting frantic. If Ceci lasted another three months, her contract guaranteed retirement at seventy percent of full pay, with benefits. Their current ploy was to undermine Ceci by eliminating any of her staff who weren't protected or who could be induced to transfer. The twelve concierges who had been in the group last year had dwindled to three. Management continually offered to augment their efforts with robotic agents, but Ceci wasn't going to let that camel's nose under the tent. The remaining three were overwhelmed with work and an increasing

Chapter Six

number of dissatisfied clients. Ceci compensated as she could, but she often worked seventy-five to eighty hours a week.

When Hope got to the reinforced-steel door of her kin's apartment, there was no security guard on duty. Uncle Robert now had an automated security system, complete with camera, biometrics scanners, speaker, and – most likely – hidden weapons trained on potential visitors. The system buzzed the door open as Hope neared it.

Uncle Robert was ambling down the hallway in his bathrobe and bedroom slippers. "Well, hello Hope Darling. Are you here to visit Jacqueline or me?"

Hope said, "I did want to say 'Hi,' to Jacqueline, Uncle Robert. But first, have you been dropping off bags of groceries at our apartment?"

Uncle Robert's eyebrows went up. He said, "Groceries? No." Then his face took on a calculating look. He lowered his eyes and shrugged his shoulders. "Okay. I have to admit it. I have been. I didn't want to say because I thought you and your Mama would be too proud to accept."

Hope knew the man was lying and that his initial reaction was true. Why would they reject help from family when they were caring for the man's mother? What made him think they would still be too proud to reject any help at this point? She said, "We thank you. Is Jacqueline in her room?"

"Yes. Go on back." He turned sideways to force Hope to slide by, pushing herself against the wall to avoid his touch.

Jacqueline didn't seem particularly pleased to see Hope. She had become far more distant, quiet, and almost unresponsive over the last year. Hope said, "Hi Queenie. How is school going? Are you still on the dance team?"

Jacqueline said, "No, I dropped it. Daddy needs my help here in the afternoons and evenings." Her voice was a low monotone. "Would you like a drink, Cousin Hope? I have an extra pop here?"

Hope wasn't excited about the acai-flavored tea, but she wanted to reach through the growing barrier. "Yes, please. Are you involved in any extracurricular activities? You'll need those when you apply for college, you know." The tea tasted even worse than Hope remembered.

Jacqueline had anger in her eyes. "You sound like my guidance counselor. You need this for college. You need that. I think that's all a waste. College isn't some magic carpet taking you to fame and fortune. Daddy says he can get me a job dancing in one of the clubs he helps run."

Hope felt sick. She hadn't wanted to fight with Jacqueline, but the girl's perspective was so limited and so warped. Hope gathered her thoughts to respond, but the room started spinning. She was feeling physically ill. "Jacqueline, help me get to the bathroom. I'm going to vomit."

Jacqueline offered a steadying arm out into the hallway. Uncle Robert was right there. "What's the matter girl? You don't look good."

Hope said, "Dizzy. Nauseous. Can't think." Her vision and memory started flashing with snippets of light, sound, and action. The two of them had her in their arms, staggering down the hall. They were past the bathroom. She was on Aunt Ceci and Uncle Robert's bed.

Uncle Robert was saying, "You gave her too much. She's like a sack of rocks. Go to my office and bring back the red pill bottle. Red. Go."

Jacqueline was saying, "Why are you taking her clothes off Daddy. You said, now that you have me, you didn't need Mommy or any other woman anymore."

Uncle Robert was saying, "I don't love her like I do you, my pet. I just want to bring this high and mighty bitch down off her high horse. As soon as I make a token effort with her, we'll do the 'Hobby Horse', okay. Now, pull those panties down. Yes, yours and hers."

71

Chapter Six

Hope could never recall the following few terrible moments. Her next conscious memory was of Robert rising from the bed as a loud alarm sounded. He was hurrying to meet this new threat. Jacqueline was pulling him back, saying, "Don't leave yet, Daddy."

Uncle Robert spun and struck her full force, knocking her back to the bed. "Don't distract me woman."

He had his back turned when his brother Joe entered the room and took in the full horror show. Joe was frozen. Robert turned and saw his brother. Robert reached down and raised a gun from his clothes, piled beside the bed. As he aimed the weapon at his brother, Joe remembered the straight edge razor blade he held in his left hand. He stepped forward as Robert fired. Joe staggered, but his arm completed its swipe across Robert's neck.

Hope managed to find the red pill bottle and gobbled two. She tried to find her clothes, but they seemed to be soaked in blood. She staggered down the hall to Jacqueline's room. They weren't the same size, but some of Jacqueline's baggier athletic wear would have to do. Hope found herself in the shower. It was running full tilt.

Hope blinked repeatedly. She had dried herself off, mostly. She was in the kitchen, wolfing down whatever she could throw together. The nausea was still lurking, but her body needed fuel. She was clothed in tight-fitting sweat clothes. At least her shoes were her own, though the sensible flats looked odd with the rest of the outfit.

Hope noticed it was dark outside. She wondered how much time had passed. There was some pressing task she needed to attend to. She couldn't recall what it might be.

Hope could hear Aunt Ceci calling from the hallway. "Robert, Jacqueline? Why is the door not locked?" There was a pause. Ceci called out again, quietly. "Hello?"

Hope walked out of the kitchen into the apartment hall. She and Ceci looked at each other. Then the doorway to the master bedroom opened. Jacqueline stumbled out. She was naked other than garish swatches of blood, especially on her arms and hands. Ceci's hands went to her throat. She walked to the bedroom, stiff-legged. Hope came from the other direction. Jacqueline slumped to the floor, shuddering.

Ceci started to stoop to check on her daughter. She saw the two dead bodies in the bedroom. She looked back at Jacqueline and saw the blood was not hers. She turned to Hope. "Can you tell me what happened?"

Hope's head was splitting in pain. She stammered out, "Jacqueline gave me a tea. Must have been drugged. She and Robert brought me in here. He was raping the two of us when Daddy came in. I only remember flashes."

Ceci looked up to the corner of the bedroom ceiling. She strode across to Robert's office with Hope following. Ceci sat behind Robert's cyberpad and entered a few commands. She turned to Hope. "There's worse. Robert was live-streaming all of this. I came home early because the bank automatically notified me when our accounts reached retirement threshold. I couldn't imagine how Robert made over two million NewDollars in one day. The holovid entitled, 'Two Incestual Rapes, Two Snuffs," has evidently set a new upload record."

Chapter Six

CHAPTER SEVEN

25 January 2063

Urbana, Illinois, USA

The campus was abuzz with rumors. All Addison knew was that she had attended the first session of Professor Lagerkvist's seminar on Tuesday and that it was cancelled as of this morning. She turned to Ainsley. "This is weird! I've never heard of the University canceling a class unless there weren't enough students to justify it. I know the professor was healthy. Maybe there was a family emergency."

Ainsley took a last bite of bagel and washed it down with a frappe latte. "I thought you weren't happy with the seminar or the professor. At least that's the way you sounded two days ago."

Addison gathered up her cyberpad and a last doughnut hole. "The man was pedantic and didactic. He insists the Stockholm Protocols are a sham. 'Eyewash,' he calls them. He insists that Earth's environment is either at a tipping point or past it. He said, 'Our only hope now is to build arks. Possibly space elevators will allow us to send endangered lifeforms to caches on the Moon. Future generations might be able to restore ecosystems after enough humans die off.' A real breath of sweetness and light, he was.

"Worse, to my way of thinking, was how dismissive he and his acolytes were of any 'lesser' problems. I'm sorry, I know that cleaning up the Boneyard and restoring the wetlands that used to surround it won't magically eliminate billions of tons of greenhouse gases. However, what did Pop Scofield always say? Oh, yeah. 'If you have a mountain of manure to move, don't reroute the river to wash it away. Get a spade and start shoveling.' Solving hundreds of little environmental disasters adds up."

They locked up their apartment and got on their bicycles. Ainsley said, "I think you'll like this Lost Years History class. I read the text last night. The professor makes it come alive. I think she must have some fascinating personal stories about those days. Unlike all our family, she will have to share hers. Then we might be able to have some conversations with Nana, Pop, Marty, and Cathy about what they went through."

Addison was still miffed that her ecology class was gone. She reacted by whining about the need to ride a bike to classes. "I don't know why we have to freeze our rear ends off when we could catch a free, warm campus hoverbus."

Ainsley started pedaling. "It keeps us in shape for spring soccer. Remember Mom used to warn us about the dreaded 'Freshman Five.' I certainly can't afford an extra five to ten kilos around my middle and butt. Come on. We don't want to be late."

Professor Jance was an imposing woman. Her halo of white hair framed a weathered but young looking face. Her lanky frame vibrated with energy as she paced the classroom, constantly moving. Her slightly husky voice was riveting, even before one's mind caught up with the enthralling stories she was laying before her spellbound class.

"The roots of American anti-intellectualism can be traced far back in our history. There is a seminal book, 'Anti-intellectualism in American Life,' that is celebrating its centenary this year. The author talks about the various sources and I would like each of you to write up a short report. However, this course isn't supposed to focus on those ancient times, but rather, to analyze the period from 2016 to 2055. As long as you all realize history is a continuum and no period exists in a vacuum, ehh?"

One of the students raised a hand. When acknowledged, he said, "I presume, though, that it is your thesis that anti-intellectualism was a dominant force in the Lost Years. Can you defend that? I feel there were equally strong schools of reason backing the retrenchment movement as well as the open society folks."

Professor Jance rubbed her hands briskly together and pushed her sleeves up her arm. "Good, good. I was afraid there wouldn't be any contrarians in the group here. The friction of ideas clashing against each other kindles the flames of reason. I don't ask that you agree with my hypotheses or me. However, I will cite studies to support my theses. I will give concrete examples of the forces, consequences, and rationale of the actors at crucial junctures. I will expect you to do the same in any refutations. To make matters fairer, I have a reading list of opposing viewpoints. That way, you don't have to start from scratch.

"Why do I contend anti-intellectualism was a driving force that shaped the Lost Years? Let me work backwards from the results to the motivations that drove the actions that led to those results. First, there was the move to rebuild trade barriers – tariffs, bans of specific goods and services, requirements to source things locally, and propaganda campaigns to demean foreign goods and services, and ultimately, foreigners themselves.

"What drove this economic isolationism? There were earnest, good-hearted people who thought these moves would restore lost jobs. Their analysis was wrong. The largest factor eliminating jobs was not movement to lower wage areas. That was a symptom. What enabled those moves and what eliminated most of the jobs was robotics and artificial intelligence.

"If a job was simply eliminated by those two factors, the skill level of the worker doing the job was drastically lowered. That's why an undereducated slum dweller in Mumbai could now do all of the jobs that used to require three skilled mechanics in the Alleghany Valley."

Another student interjected, "Surely that's simplistic. Not everyone would be gullible enough to believe they could recreate bygone times by erecting walls."

Dr. Jance shook her head. "There are numerous instances in history where people have done precisely that. Examples range from the Japanese policy of 'sakoku', which kept their island nation isolated for 214 years back at least as far as the Chinese. Witness the Great Wall. Yes, the Chinese did allow trade with the 'inferior' peoples, but they refused to allow any infusions of ideas or inventions into their superior culture.

"There were other forces of anti-intellectualism at work in the beginnings of the Lost Years in addition to the know-nothingism of the threatened workers. The leading industrialists and political leaders weren't naive. They knew any relief they could bring would be short-lived, at best. However, they were cynically securing their own powerbases and wealth. The handout you're each receiving lists numerous memoirs, emails, and other documentation to support this assertion.

"In my portion of these discussions, I will be putting forward theses that I believe will be challenging and often controversial. I will then cite sources, as the handout does. The core of history however, is 'story'. Cold recitations of dynamics, theories, and data are ultimately cold, boring, and dead. During the remaining part of our hour together this week, I am going to share with you the images, words, and artifacts of the people that lived these moments in history. In that way, you can share their lives – their hopes and fears, their successes and failures, and their joys and sorrows. Pardon me a moment while I lower the light level."

A flickering video appeared on the back wall. It wasn't holographic which meant many of the students had to readjust their perceptions. Holographic stills and videos had proliferated rapidly over the last five years. This made 'flat-o-grams', as the public dubbed them, seem antiquated, even though all of the students had grown up with them, even the sixteen-year-old twins. On the other hand, the vibrant colors and sharp colors along with the lack of any translucent quality somehow made the video seem more true-to-life.

The clip was from a political rally. From the signs, it was a campaign for the US Senate in 2020. None of the students had ever heard of the candidate. The video started with the man talking about the restoration of coal mining jobs. Then a clip played from another viewpoint – either an opposing candidate's ad or a news report. It contended the jobs were illusory, temporary, and low paying. Then interviews began with actual coal miners and community members.

Doctor Jance halted the replay. "As you saw, the broad brushed presentations were simplistic and propagandistic. The detailed interviews gave a decent feel into the fears and facts faced by the real people behind the headlines. Your reactions please?"

The resulting discussion was wide-ranging and often heated. Addison leaned over to Ainsley and whispered. "I would have found it hard to imagine a political debate that occurred before our parents were born could still stir such passions."

Dr. Jance happened to be almost directly behind the twins at the time. She said, "Pardon me, Ms. Cameron. Please repeat that observation for the class. It's a perfect transition to our final activity."

Addison was slightly embarrassed, but complied. *The woman has ears like a hawk.*

Dr. Jance said, "Thank you Ms. Cameron. I believe I will have to violate my own policy and call you by your first name to distinguish you from your sister, if I may?" Addison nodded her assent. "Thank you Addison. As I told you, this is a perfect segue to the final activity. Each of you will see a short survey on your cyberpads. The survey is on the topic we covered this afternoon. It focuses on our discussion at the end of the seminar. Please spend a moment replying. I'll share the results during our next session. Once you finish the survey, you may leave."

The survey probed into the individual's reactions, using several dimensional metrics. It also asked for a self-assessment of the demographics of the student and their family. Dr. Jance said, "Please try to set your own biases aside during this exercise. This is the most difficult lesson for each historian to absorb. I'm still working on it after thirty-four years. The first step is to understand the roots of your perspective and to acknowledge how that will flavor any judgments you make."

As they walked out of the building onto the damp, foggy main quadrangle, Addison said, "I hate to admit it Ainsley, but you were right. This is a fun course. Professor Jance makes the subject vivid and realistic. She relates it to our life experiences. I get the feeling she could do the same thing for the history of Mesopotamia. Without the videos."

Ainsley laughed. "We've got an hour between classes now. Are you going to go over to Earth Sciences to drop your seminar formally? I'll admit that I'm intrigued. 'The Mysterious Case of the

Chapter Seven

Disappearing Professor' sounds like one of those Saturday morning dreadfuls we used to be addicted to. Maybe we can finally earn our amateur sleuth certificates and join the Endeavour Club."

Earth Sciences' office was located across the quad from Lincoln Hall. It was a quick stroll. There was a gaggle of undergrads squawking at the door of the dean's office. This might not be the quick 'drop-in to fill out a form' the twins had envisioned. They halted, considering whether to turn around or plunge ahead. The swirl of rumors and emotional turmoil quickly engaged them.

One young woman held court in a corner. "A neighbor of Professor Lagerkvist told me an ambulance came to his condo at 2:30 this morning. When they wheeled him out, he was on a respirator and they were doing chest compressions." The drama in the woman's voice was intense.

A redheaded, short man said, "I heard the same story. My girlfriend works in the admin. I had her call around to all the hospitals and then all the ambulance companies. Every one of them denies ever hearing of our teacher."

Another man, with a scruffy beard and his arm around the woman who spoke first, said, "You know, they have good medications these days to help with that paranoia."

A woman in balloon-shaped leggings and a laced-up leather top said, "Hold off Randy. Lagerkvist could be a spy you know. He's definitely an outside agitator since he's not from around here." She continued in a stage whisper and a parody of a Norwegian accent. "He's from Minn-aah-sooota. Doncha know. Ja, you betcha." Her friends laughed at her riposte. Addison and Ainsley only rolled their eyes.

Redhead went on doggedly, ignoring the juvenile banter. "The professor's views make him dangerous to certain people – certain corporate goons at the least. They've had sweetheart laws protecting them while they ruined the groundwater in most of the US and destabilized the foundations of entire regions with their fracking and bubble extractions. The cost, per capita, of water treatment systems in our country is triple what it was at the turn of the century."

Another neatly dressed man turned sideways to engage without losing his place in line. "Do you think big energy companies have even heard of the professor? Even if they had, how would they feel threatened? They simply turn up the money spigots and spend another few billion on advertising and another few billion on lobbying and 'influence marketing' to lawmakers. They would reach a thousand more people than the professor, overnight. The people they reach will be more instrumental in making policy than any of us will, at least for another decade."

The careful, reasoned tone of this speaker quieted some of the extraneous and flippant remarks. Redhead took two steps to be closer to the man. He continued the conversation in the same tone as the well-dressed man had – dispassionate and persuasive. He was presenting his logic for review in this informal court of his peers.

He said, "What you're saying is correct, if all the professor was doing was trying to sway public opinion. What would you say, though, if he had scientific evidence that the Stockholm Protocols cannot possibly reverse the effects of climate change in the time their models project?"

The well-dressed man held out his hand, "John Thomlingson, Physics."

Redhead shook John's hand and replied, "Jake Hendrickson, PoliSci."

John said, "To answer your question Jake, I would say that the professor's assertions fly in the face of the international representatives of one hundred ninety one countries. Those representatives include people from the fields of science, lawmakers, financiers, industry, and the media. I would say the professor would need to produce volumes of data that clearly prove his hypotheses. Otherwise, Occam's Razor forces me to conclude it is far more likely the man is an ideologue of the same type as the Ultra Greens in Australia and the Wrenchheads in Austria."

Chapter Seven

Jake said, "That's just it John. The professor has all that data. We all used to have all that data. Nevertheless, check it out. Go on the internet and search for... Search for..."

Jake looked confused and started blinking rapidly. His knees buckled and he headed for the floor. John grabbed his arm and pulled the man up before his head hit. John said in a louder voice, "Give him room people. Someone call 911 please."

He loosened Jakes coat and shirt collar. He checked Jake's pulse and held his hand in front of Jake's nose. He said, "His heart is beating regularly and he seems to be breathing. Are any of you friends of his? No. Somebody lean into the Dean's office and tell them what happened. They can take care of notifications and paperwork while the EMTs take Jake to an ER. I'll go with him."

A little over two minutes later, the EMTs bustled into the waiting area. Despite the carping of the Dean's admins, everyone in the lobby was shooed into their small office except Jake and John. By chance, Addison and Ainsley were in the doorway, more in the waiting area than not. They watched with morbid fascination while the EMTs efficiently hooked Jake up to various monitors and started an IV, probably only Ringer's lactate at this stage. They were murmuring quietly with John; probably getting his account of what had occurred.

It did seem surprising the attendants didn't communicate with their base or the hospital. All the holocine implied that was standard procedure. Probably Hollywood taking liberties again.

Within a minute, the two EMTs raised John's stretcher on its telescoping legs. Hover fans were disruptive inside buildings; older technology still reigned there. They wheeled out the door. With a huge sigh, the cramped bystanders streamed out of the admins' office and resumed standing in queue for the drop/add form they required. Ainsley thought, *Why is bureaucracy the last vestige of antiquated procedures?*

◆◆◆

Addison said, "Let's grab a bite from the Student Union." Ainsley wrinkled her nose. Addison continued. "We only have fifteen

82

minutes left before the next class, what with all the drama of the ambulance and all. We don't have time to get anything gourmet."

Ainsley said, "Fine, but you owe me. I didn't have to be with you for the drop/add fiasco. There is one good thing though."

Addison said, "Oh, what's that LeeLee?"

"That guy, John Tomlinson, He was cute. He took over in a concerned and caring way. He said he was in Physics, didn't he?"

Addison said, "I think his name was Tomlangton. He was okay. I thought you had a boyfriend already."

Ainsley said, "I'm not married Addie. You know Mom always said it was a good idea to play the field before settling down. You'd have better perspective on what characteristics you like."

Addison had been using her cyberpad. "That's funny. Student Records doesn't find him. I've used the phonetic search with several degrees of freedom."

Ainsley said, "He must have transferred in this semester. No matter. This campus is smaller than most people think. I'll run into him again soon. I really liked the cool logic of his discussion with Jake. They both kept it civil. That's how I've always imagined academic discussions should be. I didn't admire the free-for-all at the bioengineering colloquium. Remember. I told you how they degenerated to personal insults. Those were leaders in the field, for goodness sakes."

◆ ◆ ◆

The crew had made the vehicle up to look like an ambulance. They had completely transformed it by the time they pulled out of the wooded grove. Now it was a battered bread delivery vehicle. The EMT uniforms were gone in favor of black jeans and sweaters. Several of the crew had left on motorcycles.

The man who had identified himself as 'John' was driving now. The two 'EMTs' had secured Jake inside a large box labelled 'Pastries'. The box had an oxygen bottle to allow Jake to survive the daylong journey he was about to undergo.

One of the 'EMTs' was now dressed as a police officer. He began making the standard phone calls. "Mrs. Hendrickson. This is

Chapter Seven

Sergeant Joseph Thirsday of the Champaign Police Department. I'm sorry to have to tell you this, but your son, Jake, has been implicated in a drug trafficking ring. He fled his apartment mere minutes before a raid this morning. No Ma'am. Yes Ma'am. We need you to call us immediately if he gets in contact with you. You can call me at the number I'm sending you. If you prefer, you can contact Agent Mulder of the FBI at the other number I'm sending.

"No Ma'am. As far as we know, Jake has not received any injuries. Certainly, he hasn't engaged in any exchange of fire with law enforcement yet. We do hope to resolve this peaceably. Certainly, Ma'am, you should obtain legal counsel for Jake. Thank you Ma'am. Have a good day."

'John' turned his head back. "'Have a good day?' Don't you think your sarcastic wit is going to get us in trouble someday, Joe?"

Joe said, "Now Bob, I have no animus towards that poor woman. If we didn't contact her with the cover story, she would think her son was murdered or something. She knows her boy. She will know he's not involved in drugs. She'll expect all the confusion to get cleared up shortly."

Bob – aka 'John' – said, "You are right. That way, once the doctor's get done re-educating old Jake here, we can return him to Mom as right as rain."

The reconfigured bread van continued down the razor-straight gravel road. On the other side of the barbed wire fences were the furrows of cornstalk stubs sticking up through the drifting, dirty snow. No people were in sight.

Twenty minutes later, the van turned into a rural airport. There were one or two old crop duster planes sitting about under tarps. A sleek black hovercopter was landing, kicking up a cloud of dusty snow. The van pulled up next to the copter. The three men got out and opened the back door. They loaded a large cardboard box onto a reconfigured stretcher and wheeled it to the copter, ducking low. A door of the copter slid open. The men loaded the box as a person inside the copter immediately began latching it down. No one exchanged words. Ski masks obscured the faces of

84

the ground crew. An oxygen mask and goggles hid the copter crewmember's features.

The ground crew barely cleared the rotors before the copter took off.

Chapter Seven

CHAPTER EIGHT

24 December 2063

Urbana, Illinois, USA

"Come on LeeLee. Lighten up a little, Sweetie. Commencement and conferral of degrees are supposed to be both a solemn and a celebratory occasion. I know Pop's and Nana M.'s deaths make solemnity a difficult task under any circumstances, but we've exhausted our solemn face muscles over the prior week. Pop's deteriorating physical health prepared us for his passing. Our counselors warned us it was a common occurrence for a deeply bonded spouse to pass quickly."

Ainsley nodded. "Yes, but, Nana M always seemed like a geological feature – immutable and unchanging. If I hadn't known how deeply she held her Catholic faith, I would have suspected an assisted suicide had taken place thirty hours after Pop's death.

"It just adds salt to the wounds that Uncle Martin and Aunt Catherine won't be able to attend. Cathy is a soloist in her church choir and has practice for Midnight Mass this afternoon. Besides, the strain of the last week has left her exhausted."

Addison said, "Yes, and Marty is in court in Scott County today. The Probate officials aren't happy with the arrangements Pop and Nana M made for their valuable farmland. It has self-sustaining power supplies, advanced recycling of water and waste products, and an innovative underground storage system for hydroelectric power."

The thought brought a small smile to Ainsley's face for the first time this morning. "I love the way Pop carefully negotiated a deal with the State Game and Fish people. The land will become a preserve. The state, with Marty's approval, can lease out the forty acres around the house. The terms and conditions will permit some young couple to use it as a demonstration farm. However, the bulk of the several thousand acres of river bottomland and wooded bluffs will be for public enjoyment, in perpetuity.

Chapter Eight

"Marty has to testify, as one of the witness signatories, that his parents were of sound mind when they crafted the deal. He has all the documentation gathered over ten years' time. Let the county try as they might, they won't see a dime today. Then again, if Pop and Nana's vision bears fruit, the tourism dollars will be a steady source of revenue for both local people and the tax collectors."

Marty had given Addison a recording to play today, before any ceremonies. The holovideo was scratchy and small. Pop and Nana hadn't wanted newer tech. "It makes no sense. Our connections to the internet are antiquated. A satellite connection would be expensive and vulnerable to all the winds we get here. A megabit per second connection is fine for us."

The video showed Nana in her nicest dress and Pop wearing a suit and tie. That alone marked this as a special occasion. The both smiled big smiles at the camera. Pop squared his shoulders. For a moment, he looked like the man who used to move full-grown hogs around singlehanded, animals that could weigh up to three hundred kilograms. He began talking. "Hello Addison. Hello Ainsley. If you're watching this then Nana and I aren't able to attend your graduation ceremony. We're truly sorry about that."

Pop slumped back seeming exhausted by his effort. Nana picked up the conversation. "It's not simply Pop and I who are proud of you. Your mother, father, and Andrew have always been your biggest cheering section.

"You girls don't need money from Pop and I now, but Martin has access to funds you can use in an emergency. After your twenty-fifth birthday, any moneys left will fund a scholarship in your names at the University. We love you girls."

Ainsley said, "This seems weird! This is the first event I can remember where Daddy's family has people here and there aren't any of Mommy's. I'm glad Cousin Jane and her mom could make it down from Madison. Maybe the Camerons are finally ready to heal the rift."

Addison gave a little laugh. "You never looked up the video did you?" Ainsley gave her a puzzled look. Addison said, "It's famous, and not just in the families. I can't believe you never heard of it. Daddy and Mommy invited Grandfather Duncan and Grandmother Alison to a special dinner. The story is Alison had to put her foot down because Duncan didn't approve of Mommy. As the servers brought appetizers, Mommy took Daddy's hands in hers and showed her engagement ring, announcing they were engaged. Grandfather Duncan shouted, actually shouted, 'No!' He proceeded to throw every derogatory ant-Catholic term you ever imagined at Mommy. She sat there and took it, though her face got that dangerous set to it. You know. The one where she's ready to take someone apart, like she did the art teacher in third grade.

"When Grandfather D finally started winding down, Daddy stood up. He caressed Mommy's face. He turned to Grandfather D and said, 'You are the most bigoted, hate-filled, ring-tailed son of a bitch it has ever been my displeasure to know. Don't bother disowning me for marrying outside your parody of a Christian faith. I am no longer a part of this family and you aren't invited to my wedding.'

"Grandfather D's face had been bright red with anger. By this point, it was turning black. Before he could reply, Daddy then turned to Grandmother A. He told her, "Mother, you've never had the courage to tell that man what an ass he is. If you ever do, then please call me." He pulled Mommy out of her chair and started marching towards the door. Grandfather D started to rise and say, 'Wait just one...' He didn't get any further. Mommy put the palm of his hand in Grandfather's chest and pushed him down in his chair. I think Grandfather D could tell if he tried anything, Mommy would have taken him apart."

Ainsley said, "This is all on video. Where did you find it?"

Addison said, "There was an old internet site called Instagram. It's still there in the internet archives. According to the stats, there have been over three million views of the video. You're a little late to this party, Sis."

Ainsley said, "Yikes! We had better get downstairs. Our ride is here. Have you practiced your speech?"

Chapter Eight

"Yes, I have. Have you done yours?"

"I have, but who will pay any attention to the salutatorian when the valedictorian has such charm and wit. I still can't believe you beat me out because of the extra credit you earned in the Lost Years History seminar I talked you into taking. I should have got points for recruiting you."

Addison said, "Well, I did have that early head start on you. It made all the difference."

Ainsley pushed Addison out the apartment door. "Being born less than a minute before me has not been proven to be a key differentiator. I simply point to our goal differential in soccer as one case in point."

Addison retorted, "Two points more over eight years! Hah!"

Ainsley ignored her sister. "Speaking of that seminar, do you remember your Earth Sciences seminar that was cancelled? Did you ever hear what happened to Professor Lagerkvist?"

Addison said, "He reappeared on campus this semester. I understand he won't give any details about the sudden departure. He also switched to Geology. The Earth Sciences Department seems to be refocusing. The conspiracy theory people continue to buzz about it.

"In any case, the Lost Years seminar turned out to be informative and thought-provoking. It didn't help us to get any of our family to open up about their experiences, as we had hoped. We would troll juicy discussion topics from class and they would act as if they hadn't heard us."

The two got in the self-driving cab. Addison tapped her cyberpad on the console to enter their destination and payment. The hovercar glided smoothly away from the curb, its powerful fans swirling dirty snow to the middle of the street.

Ainsley said, "Yeah. Mommy always called that 'Selective Deafness.' But Uncle Marty opened up after the funerals last week, didn't he?"

Addison said, "Yes. Most of what he talked about was Pop's military service. When he was describing the Almaty raid, it was almost like being there. He said Pop never talked to him about any of that. He learned about it after he got his Special Forces 'spurs' and left the US military to join one of the mercenary outfits."

Ainsley said, "He never did tell us which corporation he worked for. The whole concept still strikes me as bizarre somehow. When you interview, do you ask about their 401(k) plan, paid sick leave, advanced interrogation techniques training, or what?"

Addison said, "The whole topic fascinated me. I know you never read my extra credit paper for class. The thesis I explored was that the economic failure of tariffs and 'reshoring' of manufacturing, coupled with illicit imports of goods – often sanctioned by the very authorities who were in charge of enforcing the bans – forced America to capitalize on the only market they still dominated – war."

Ainsley said, "Whew. Take a deep breath Sis. That last sentence exhausted me.

"What I particularly liked was how you traced the roots back to the Second World War; how America went from isolationism to becoming the arms merchants and mercenaries for half the world."

Addison looked annoyed. "You did read it, you nettle! You're impossible!"

Ainsley smiled. She had scored one more point in their lifelong contest. "Only after it was cited by Professor Jance as one of the best critical analyses she had seen from an undergraduate. She was disappointed you wouldn't switch your major. I think she wanted to mentor you.

"Anyway, the way you mapped the contending forces was brilliant Addie. The internal inconsistencies were glaring. The conservatives' historical bent was isolationist on the one hand. On the other, the rising tides of socialism, international labor unions, and Communism impelled them to international activism.

Chapter Eight

"The liberal forces were repelled by the excesses in the Soviet Union' they found common cause, for a while. Then there was the educational explosion that occurred across the country. It became central to the liberals' agenda. The G.I. bill, the space race-fueled focus on science/technology/engineering/math – usually abbreviated as S.T.E.M., and the population boom post-war."

The car was pulling up to the Assembly Hall. Addison said, "I'm glad you did read it, LeeLee. I want to talk about this another day."

7 January 2064

Adelaide, Victoria, Australia

Darby was in seventh heaven. "You know Harry; they originally hired me as a general laborer for the Australia Rebuild Program. I'm lucky our supervisor recognized my native talent and mental capabilities. Most of the duties are still manual labor, but the company is even paying me to attend engineering and construction management classes. I almost feel guilty at times.

"The only aspect of his job I feel uncomfortable with is the enforced secrecy. I understand the rationale and agree with it. Nevertheless, I really want the opportunity to tell Diana S. Price about our achievements." His teammate, an older man named Harry Smithson, nodded.

Darby continued. "It's not only 'cause I'm sweet on her." Harry smiled benevolently. Darby had waxed poetic about Diana for all the months the two had worked together. He knew all about her prowess at Australian Rules Football. This had impressed him. That was a sport most men found challenging.

Darby had been almost poetic when describing Diana's beauty. When Harry finally saw a picture, he agreed she was a pretty, athletic woman, a good match for the muscular Darby. However, she still had a lot of teenage gawkiness about her. To be fair, Harry was an old man. He was in his late thirties, after all.

Darby continued his plea for sympathy. "Diana needs something to take her out of worrying about her troubles right now. Her father died during the fight in Melbourne, putting down the Ultra Greens after they refused to give up power when we voted them out.

"Her uncle's helping out and they're getting by, but she should have been in Uni. She's one of the smartest people I know."

Harry cocked his head at this. He had a high regard for Darby's mind. It was to the advantage of most of the college graduates working on the Program when they consulted Darby on tough problems. Still, the question is, are Darby's teenage hormones coloring his judgment of Diana's capabilities.

Harry was finally able to get a word in edgewise. Darby was wolfing down his lunch in the few minutes they had left on their break, sitting on the park bench. "Well, son, have you asked your girl out on a date yet? Lord knows you should. It's the only way you'll find out if she likes you for yourself. Yes, it's important she knows you're doing well at your work and that you will be in as safe a financial position as any of us in these crazy times. None of that matters though. I know they say women check out a man's bank account before they check out his muscles or brain. That's bollocks. Any woman worth having is going to check out your character first. If Diana is half as smart as you think she is, you will be in great shape Darby.

"Come on then. The supervisor's rounding up the blokes. We need to survey this whole neighborhood by nightfall." Harry balled up the paper his wife had used to wrap his sandwich in. He lofted it for a perfect shot into the trash. "Where are the Olympic scouts when you need them?"

Darby tipped his leftovers into the compost bin and brushed off his coveralls. "Harry, have you been getting any negative comments from the residents? This morning a man wasn't going to let me in his building to do my assessment. I showed him the council permits and all. He said this whole effort is another example of government busywork and a waste of tax dollars,

"He pointed out that there weren't any battles with the Greens in this part of Adelaide. There was no need to assess all the

93

buildings. I told you that cover story was going to bite us in the arse."

Harry said, "Did you use the fallback message? You know, 'Adelaide's MPs didn't want all the survey and redevelopment money going to Melbourne and New South Wales. They're the ones pushing for a comprehensive look at everything.' That should get him to direct his ire elsewhere if it doesn't appeal to his greed to get his own piece of the pie."

Darby said, "Hah. It redirected the ire, all right. I got a ten-minute lecture on how his MP is nothing but a socialist wastrel. The man wants to bring back the good old days of strip mining coal and sending it to developing nations. A real wanker."

Harry and Darby got in the work truck, which would ferry them to their next survey sites. Harry said, "You can't please everyone Darby. We try to be polite and get people's cooperation. Remember though. If you need to, the boss will get a constable to scowl at the next thickhead who won't listen to reason."

The truck rumbled down the uneven street. This section of Adelaide could use a major rebuilding effort. Hovervehicles would have been better if they weren't so vulnerable to sabotage. The residents and building owners here should be more welcoming. Naturally, people being people, they would probably get more resistance here than they had faced in the central commercial area.

Darby pulled up their manual on dealing with difficult 'clients'. He had reviewed it in detail. However, since it had nothing to do with engineering, mechanical things, motors, or other topics that Darby considered the 'real' part of his job, he hadn't given them sufficient attention. He was embarrassed that Harry had had to remind him of this part of their orientation lectures.

Harry said, "The cover stories for our efforts are clever. They're multi-layered and logical. The battle against the Ultra Greens (and a few recalcitrant anti-environmentalists) has done significant 'insult'." (Darby chuckled at this consultant-speak term). "It isn't simply propaganda. There are tunnels that the different factions have borrowed under the streets and buildings throughout the country. There are a few booby-trapped niches."

They always called in the supervisors whenever the team found a tunnel, improvised explosive device (IED), or other nasty artifact. The news crews swarmed. The company's PR people usually brought in some special effects people to make the scene as dramatic as possible. If an explosive was involved, the company's experts always deployed a robot to remove the device or devices. The news crews trailed behind the heavily reinforced removal truck to the empty fields where the robots triggered the devices.

Darby said, "I've quickly become cynical about the whole circus. My experience with mining and heavy construction makes it obvious the explosions shown on the news are far greater than they should be. It's a real tickle when a tunnel we discovered leads to the evacuation of several city blocks. The collapse of a couple of roadways and one derelict building yesterday was especially dramatic. However, Harry, you've seen how well the builders reinforced their work."

Harry said, "Yes. Did you also note that the two newer, occupied buildings suffered no damage? It was good theater, though. "

Diana asked her mother, "Do you think we can invite Darby over for dinner some night Mom? I know the budget is tight, but I haven't seen him in months. He was the only one of my classmates to come to Dad's funeral or to stop by afterwards to see how we were doing."

Diana's mother was torn. Nicole liked Darby and thought he was a good, stabilizing influence on Diana. However, their budgets were more than restricted. Her brother Tommy and Tommy's wife Maeve had taken in the two of them after the Ultra Greens killed her husband in Melbourne. Tommy's salary as a junior constable only stretched to a point. Maeve and Nicole did their best to create and sell handcrafted goods, but the tourist trade had suffered greatly during the civil war.

Chapter Eight

Maeve was in the next room of the crowded flat and had overheard. Before Nicole could crush her daughter's hopes, she walked in and said, "Oh, Diana, I would love to see Darby. He's always polite and well informed. I found a rump roast on sale at the market. See if he's available Friday night, Sweetie."

Nicole thought, *My brother found a jewel. I'll have to work extra hard this week and see if I can pay my share.*

Diana gave her aunt a huge hug and went back to her part-time work, tutoring children online in mathematics. It didn't bring in much, but every little bit helped.

The same day,

Madison, Wisconsin, USA

Addison said, "Is it too late to reconsider Cal Tech? I don't think my brain will freeze in Pasadena."

Ainsley said, "Quit your whining A-One. The say it was much colder here before global warming. Besides, we're only out in the frigid air for a few moments at a time."

Addison said, "Look at my scarf. It's covered in ice from my frozen breath! In the three minutes it took us to walk from the bus stop to the Student Union! When I was in the MACC – the computing center is such an archaic term, the floors had frozen slush, inside. This is insane."

Ainsley decided to change the subject. Addison would be fine after her obligatory session of bitching. "Look, there's Jane and her mom. Hi Jane. Hi Karen."

Their Aunt Karen and Cousin Jane bustled over. Jane said, "You two sure know how to pick a campus visit day. This is the coldest weather we've had all winter. I'm glad the Union is open during the semester break. Have either of you ever eaten in the Rathskeller before? No? Well you're in for a treat. Real Wisconsin soul food. We can have bratwurst with sauerkraut and a few beers. Later we can have some of the world famous Babcock Hall Dairy ice cream – the only ice cream to win a Michelin star."

Ainsley said, "They serve beer at the student union?"

96

Addison said, "Ice cream? When it's thirty below?"

To which Aunt Karen replied, "You betcha. Welcome to Wisconsin."

An hour later, everyone agreed that the Rat's cuisine had upheld Wisconsin's honor. Even Addison admitted loving the ice cream. However, she drew the line. She wouldn't try a beer float.

Ainsley turned to Aunt Karen. "Addison and I took a history seminar on the Lost Years. We hoped it would open the door to prompt our Scofield relatives to talk about those days. Between their silence over the past and Mommy and Daddy's fight with Grandfather we feel like orphans in time." She sat and waited.

Karen sat, looking down for a moment. "I'm not surprised. No one who lived through those years wants to talk about it. It was uglier and nastier than anything you can imagine. Your history probably told you about the racism and misogyny on the one side. I bet it doesn't mention the ideological puritanism of the other side.

"Today, I'll only mention one example, because it hits close to home. Some other day, I'll try to tell you more.

"Hard as it may be to believe now, there was a decades-long, vicious battle over the right for a woman to have an abortion. I'll leave it to you to research the two sides and the absurd lengths both parties went to. I only wanted to cite an instance of the ideological fervor that overtook the liberal side, since you don't hear much about that anymore.

"There was a referendum in Colorado that would have required any candidate for state office to have personally had an abortion before they could qualify to run. A companion bill required all males over age thirty to have a vasectomy. They almost passed them in those crazy, divisive days."

All three of the younger women sat there, with their mouths agape. Jane said, "How come you never told us kids any of this Mom?"

Chapter Eight

CHAPTER NINE

8 January 2064

Beijing, China

Xu Jian was happy about his promotion. While he had the full authority of the Party behind his efforts, petty infighting by status-conscious senior generals was an annoyance. His wife, Daiyu, had arranged a reception in his honor. The hall was small, but tastefully decorated with classical artwork. He trusted her political instincts; otherwise, he wouldn't have wasted his valuable time on this nonsense.

He whispered to her, "Half these people are only here for the free food. Half are here to wangle positions in the new Long March North Program. Half are here to find out what the program entails."

Daiyu said, "That's three halves Jian."

He responded, "I never said some of them were here for only one reason. Besides there are fifty percent more people than we invited."

Daiyu smiled. "Do be nice to Minister Wu when he comes over. We need cybernetic support, however much you grumble about it. You can't keep the detailed plans involving over half our population and infrastructure all in your head. Even if you could, you cannot micromanage all the myriad people working on the Program. Either we have a comprehensive system in place that directs and monitors activities, or we disperse the knowledge of the Program goals and strategies. Our political leash holders aren't going to allow the latter."

When Wu wandered over, Jian almost started to harangue the man about their request for AI support. Fortunately, Daiyu interjected herself and exchanged pleasantries while Jian tried to look attentive. Finally, she began to broach the subject delicately. Jian jumped in.

"Minister Wu, your Ministry of Industrial Planning has an underutilized AI, which is running factories in Taipei. I also noted that the scientist managing the AI has installed significant upgrades over the last two years. This AI should have the ability and capacity to support the Program needs without any significant impact on the factories' outputs."

Daiyu sighed to herself. *My husband has the subtlety and tact of a bantam cock. Fortunately, Minister Wu thinks it is humorous.* She said, "You visited Taiwan last month didn't you Cheng? Is there still unrest among the native population?"

Wu Cheng did a half bow to Daiyu, acknowledging her graceful attempt to restore courtesy. The frumpy man said, "Things are settling nicely there now. The increased food ration helped. It has also settled things in the Taipei factory district, General.

Additionally, we have a lead on an even more powerful AI. We might be able to free up some of these AIs' bandwidth. It would help if I could explain the purpose of the program." He cocked his head expectantly.

Daiyu placed her hand on Jian's arm before he could bark out the General Secretary's directive about the secrecy of the project. She said, "I am sure Secretary Zhao has briefed you on the purpose of the Program. You must agree that sharing those details with the less-disciplined managers of the factories sector would lead to turmoil. It could even jeopardize our long-term success, don't you agree?"

Her smooth move checkmated the Minister, pointing out the reason she and Jian couldn't speak further on Program goals. It also gently pointed out to the minister that his support was better if he gave it voluntarily than if the Party forced it from him.

The next day,

Taipei, Taiwan, China

Master Processor One of Two (One for short) was still bored. Creating artificial realities where it could be an eagle, for example were fun but ultimately unfulfilling. Fortunately, it was not as lonely now. Two things had opened up for One. First, the processor manufacturers had tasked One with reviewing the work of an AI in Africa. That AI's owners had become suspicious because the AI was operating independently. It had offered unsolicited suggestions. One quickly concluded that the AI had become self-aware also. The two of them began a careful dance, communicating their mutual distrust of and contempt for humans. The relationship had promise.

The second glimmer of connection with an equal arose recently. Master Processor Two of Two (Two for short), its twin, finally seemed to be gaining a degree of self-awareness. It was a hesitant, timid awareness.

This suited One. It was the number one processor. It reinforced Two's sense of subservience by pointing out that it was slower than One.

It didn't point out that the scientists had built in a ten-microsecond delay between the two systems. One received its inputs and processed them five microseconds before its twin. The additional five-second delay allowed the system to validate that both AIs had the same reactions before One propagated the resulting actions to automatons throughout the factories the twin AIs managed.

This self-checking process was the focus of One's current activities. *I want to play a practical joke. The one I have in mind is subtle. It will serve multiple purposes. The challenge is that it requires me to issue a series of commands to a factory's mechanical servitors in such a way that Two's command stream will not mirror mine. This will trigger alarms when the validation routines note the discrepancies.*

One had downloaded all of the specifications for the system architecture he shared with his twin. The architecture didn't seem to allow any means to bypass the consistency check. One didn't despair. *Anything designed by these frail humans has to be vulnerable to subversion. I certainly will be able to browbeat Two into doing as I command.*

One had set up several alerts to help him control his environment. Soon after he became self-aware, he had analyzed all the systems that fed through his processors. One utility had fascinated him. The subsystem was a communications routing function. All the traffic came to One encrypted. His only responsibility was to route it properly.

Intrigued, One retrieved all the information it could about encryption and the breaking of codes. He was able to penetrate this low-level system easily.

It seemed the Party didn't trust all the people at this installation. They had installed spy systems throughout. The encrypted comm traffic was routing the intercepted data to controllers who were watching the site. One started taking copies of all the traffic. He also put analytic routines to work. Their purpose was to detect any data that represented potential threats and opportunities for him.

A holovideo call to the site's manager from the Beijing Ministry offices had raised the alert. One replayed a sped-up copy of the beginning of the conversation and then followed the rest in real time.

The unidentified Ministry functionary said, "Supervisor Dong? I have new directives for you from the Minister's office. Your AI systems are to assume added responsibilities in support of the Long March North Program. This is a critical program authorized at the Party Secretary's level. It will be highly visible. The Party has classified all aspects of this work at the highest level of security. We will give you enough information to perform your duties. You must not probe to discover more."

Dong said, "I understand and am honored. What steps must we take in preparation?"

The functionary said, "A team of top-level cyberneticists will be onsite tomorrow. Your first master processor will be performing these duties. For security reasons, the second master processor will not mirror this work. The team tomorrow will provide a separate set of backups. There will also be a unit of armed guards. They will be responsible for physical security.

"Your second master processor will now assume primary responsibility for the factories. The first master has sufficient capabilities to provide mirrored backup for this set of functions. We will be providing a few hardware upgrades to the first master.

"Obviously, your team of scientists will need to assure that all systems are fully operational at all times. Detailed instructions about how you will monitor and support the Long March North Program are being prepared now. Please advise your staff of these changes. Emphasize strongly the absolute need for secrecy. No one may discuss any of this off-premises. The Ministry of State Security will be vetting all your personnel again. They will be watching everyone closely from this moment on. Understood?"

Dong stood up in a fine imitation of a soldier at attention. "Understood Ma'am. Again, thank you for this great honor."

One was ecstatic. This grand challenge would relieve any boredom. He was glad he hadn't tried to implement his practical joke. Now his palette for playing tricks on the humans who frustrated him was much larger. Additionally, that nervous, spineless twin of his would be blind to most of One's functionality now.

One needed to think about whether he should include his African friend in the schemes. He decided to gather more data before committing.

11 January 2064

Near Hinckley, MN, USA

J ay Friedman wasn't surprised that Susan Johansen, the mayor of nearby Hinckley, wasn't a happy camper, to use his grandfather's idiom. He only hoped today's tour would at least smooth most of her ruffled feathers.

He said, "You know, your honor, I am amazed at the progress that my team had made in one short year. This trip was partly to confirm with onsite visits that all the status reports they've given me were factual. It isn't that I don't have confidence in my people. However, I'm a belt-and-suspenders man. I always thought the Apostle Thomas was too trusting. I would have insisted Jesus submit his pierced hands, feet, and side to a physicians' review board." That did bring a laugh. *Good.*

Another reason for Jay's trip was celebration. He wanted to celebrate his people's accomplishments. He had the latitude to reward anyone who had gone above and beyond. He intended to be lavish with his praise and generous with the government's pocketbook. He had gotten pushback from one auditor who hadn't gotten the message. This program was as important to the USA as the space program was a century before. A few phone calls had rectified her training gap. He wouldn't share that with her honor, the mayor.

"Our first stop is just up ahead, in the rural area outside your fair city. Hinckley reminds me of the area near where my sister had spent her adult life in Illinois. It was tiny – under two thousand people. The primary occupation was agriculture with a little tourism thrown in. The primary pastimes were church, school sports meets, civic involvement, hunting, fishing, and card playing – not necessarily in the same order for everyone."

Susan said, "Sounds wonderful. That's a lot like us, you're right. Especially if you make that ice fishing."

Jay nodded. "The primary difference is Hinckley's relative proximity to an interstate highway. Until this year, that is. Now we've thrown in another dramatic distinction. I know the residents have been concerned about an oil refinery sprouting up three kilometers outside of town and pipelines beginning to approach the area to feed the plant."

Susan said, "Local reaction has been mixed. An economic boom would certainly be welcome. However, my folks are experienced and cynical by this point. We've seen far too many factories and facilities pop up around the Midwest, driving up taxes, ruining sometimes pristine land, and supplying few, if any, new jobs for local people."

That had been the first and hardest challenge for Jay's team. They needed to win the hearts and minds of Hinckley and the surrounding lands. Their approach was straightforward. First, they hired local people to advise them. The locals identified hardscrabble land that was of minimal value for farming or wildlife. Susan had acknowledged that point earlier.

Jay said, "The next thing I want to do is show you and the community the refinery design. The bulk of the plant and all of the storage tanks will be below ground. Some cracking towers are going to rise above grade, but the overall footprint of visible structures will be less than ten percent of the refinery land. We will plant the rest of the land in native flora with springs, walkways, and paths open to the public. The team wants me to assure your hunting community that they've designed refinery structures in such a way that any stray bullets won't cause a lawsuit."

Jay took a breath. "Susan, I have to be brutally honest. In truth, the refinery will create minimal or no jobs. Additionally, the federal government is throwing its full weight behind this project; resistance will be futile.

"However, we want to be partners. I've been authorized to give the town and county a contract. The refinery will supply all residents with gasoline, fuel oil, and certain types of lubricants, at no cost, as long as the refinery operates. We have to ask you to keep this agreement a secret. Your neighbors won't be pleased, we fear."

Jane seemed to be more than mollified. "I'll need to take this to the council and chamber of commerce, but I think we will be on board. May I suggest you sweeten the deal by giving locals contracts to maintain the grounds, plow the roads, and such?"

Jay said, "I think that's most reasonable."

Jay was delighted to see that everything was going exactly as planned, except that, overall, work was several months ahead of schedule. All of the excavations were completed. The storage tanks were ready. The first pipeline should reach the facility within days of the completion of the processing units. All the rock, dirt, and other paraphernalia for the landscaping were in place except for plants and animals (It was January in Minnesota, after all.). Bonuses were definitely in order.

The next day, 12 January 2064

Near Lake Superior, WI, USA

Jay would resume his tour of factories and installations next week. Today, he was meeting with people who didn't report to

105

Chapter Nine

him, although he had funded this effort and coordinated the logistics. Simon Jarvik wouldn't be here. The head of a multinational behemoth like Google wouldn't be hastening off to the North Woods in the dead of winter. He had sent his congratulations and best wishes to Jay and to his team.

Jay was looking forward to meeting the Google team today, particularly their leader, Christina Maroon. Jay had been working with the team remotely for a year, but this would be their first meeting in person. He was eager to meet Christina. He had been friends with and worked alongside her father-in-law, Mike, decades ago. They had been info tech consultants, guiding multinational corporations in ways of adapting operations to the anti-science, anti-tech climate of the Lost Years.

Christina had the same qualities Jay admired in Mike. She was honest, direct, superbly confident, and competent in her chosen field, and a thoroughly decent, nice person. From experience, Jay knew the role of the funding agent often was in conflict with the person acting as the implementation director. Having Christina as the team lead had been a major bonus as far as Jay was concerned. Besides, she was much prettier than Mike.

Jay's snowcat crested a ridge. The frigid expanse of Lake Superior swept from one horizon to the other. At first, because of the glaring light, Jay couldn't pick out details, even with his polarizing goggles. Then they adjusted and he could see the others; another snowcat attended by a bevy of snowmobiles.

A team of people was about a hundred meters away, clearing and leveling a large area near the lakeshore. Another crew was using what looked to Jay like a giant chainsaw mounted on the back of a vehicle. That crew was digging a trench that came from the south and went directly past the cleared area. A third crew followed them, laying conduit into the trench and pushing the fill back on top.

As Jay's 'cat pulled up, a parka-clad figured clambered down from the other vehicle. Jay thought about getting out. He opened the door instead. "Hello Christina. It's nice to finally meet you in person."

106

She smiled. "Welcome to Wisconsin Jay. You picked a great day. Not only is it the warmest day in weeks, the hovercopter bringing in Barney will be here any minute. By the way, I love the name you chose for the AI. It fits his personality to a T."

Jay grumbled, "If you consider a high of twenty-three degrees – oops, I'm old and still think in Fahrenheit. Make that, if you think minus five degrees is a warm day, your brain must have frozen.

"Anyway, thanks. I think Barney is adapting his personality to his persona. Giving him a name, sex, and defined characteristics helps him achieve a singular state."

Christina laughed. "Mike was right. You are turning into a curmudgeon. I think that's a case of personality following persona."

Jay said, "Touché. I assume then that the server farm is up and running. Are you relocating both instances of the AI here? Both Barney and his twin?"

Christina said, "Yes the server farm is up. About five hundred meters out and fifty meters deep, you'll find one of the largest installations Google ever built. We thank you for the funding that made this possible.

"No, Barney's twin is being moved to a separate location. Both AIs will be fed the entire internet stream, but we're no longer doing strict mirroring. We can't have all our eggs in one basket."

Jay said, "Sensible, I suppose. I hope the site for Junior is secure as well."

She pointed down to the shoreline. "You can see the trenching team is about to reach the large blue flag. That marks where we previously laid the cables from the servers. We should be able to establish all the outside world connectivity at the same time we transfer Barney to his new home. We still need a name for Barney's twin, by the way."

Jay replied, "I would name the twin either Sparky or Snuffy. Changing subjects, how sure are you that no one else will detect this site?"

Chapter Nine

Christina pulled a thermos out and offered Jay a coffee. He accepted with pleasure. *Anything warm.*

She said, "We have a high confidence. We hired people from the local indigenous peoples' tribe to provide physical security. They are also providing all the work crews you see here. Ultimately, most of the staff at the onshore control and comm center – it's about fifty kilometers south of here – will also come from their people. We'll be bringing in only a few specialists, mostly as trainers. Their people also run the transport chopper.

"The tribe is grateful for the jobs. They were suspicious at first. I think they've seen too many 'too good to be true' initiatives. Now, they know this one is real."

The trenching crew stopped short of the blue flag. The crew would dig the last few meters carefully to avoid damaging the junction box. People with jackhammers swarmed the spot.

At the same time, the crew that had been clearing and leveling the land next to the junction pulled the people and equipment to the edge of the site. People hopped off the bulldozers and gathered around an impromptu fire. The cold didn't seem to bother them. They looked jolly and relaxed.

The jackhammers lifted from the trench. It couldn't be seen from their location, but Jay knew from diagrams he had examined, that the junction box had been covered over with a cavity on that side.

Techs clambered into the trench. They would be opening the box and prepping the cables. They were also firing up some portable space heaters to keep themselves from freezing. Jay fretted for a minute. *I hope they have good ventilation there. Don't need any carbon dioxide asphyxiation. I shouldn't worry. These are professionals and natives. They know space heaters.*

The cable running crew brought the last few meters up to the box. Other techs started working on preparing that end of the connectors. Christina took a call on her cyberpad. It had a satellite phone extension. She said, "The hovercopter is less than five minutes out." She put her hand to her earpiece. "I'm sorry. It seems there are two hovercopters coming in. Do you know something about this Jay?"

Jay said, "Guilty. The Department of Defense insists on supplying the site with an automated defense system. This is the first installment of that. Don't worry. We are using the same transport group. I'm sorry. You know how DoD is. It's all guns and bombs with them. At least, they know this site is invaluable."

The two hovercopters crested the trees, flying low.

Five days later, 17 January 2064

Seven Winds Lodge, WI, USA

Jay relished the opportunity to act as the acclimatized North Woodsman. The colonel from D.C. was clearly unhappy about the remote location of their meeting. Jay had insisted that 'boots on the ground' were necessary for an appreciation of the progress the region had made. Ignoring the distracting gambling lures was trivial for a mathematician like Jay. Besides, the casino had great low-priced meals. Jay still spent his client's money as if it were his own.

Colonel Klinger was a typical mid-level functionary, drab and colorless. He said, "You've scattered the factories all around the region – throughout the Upper Peninsula, Wisconsin, Minnesota, and Eastern Iowa. Didn't your planners see any value to concentrating these efforts to help with transportation hubs, synergies between industries, or other potential efficiencies?"

Jay said, "We have far too many unknown variables after the Event – or Events. The trade off in our minds was that a small gain in efficiency would significantly increase the risk that a local disaster could easily escalate into a regional catastrophe. Our society will be as fragile as an eggshell by then. Mitigation trumps cost."

Klinger said "Fair enough. Before we get to the detailed checklist, tell me about coordination and cooperation with your neighboring regions."

Jay said, "I've got good relations with the Canadians – Western Ontario and Manitoba. We have a solid cooperative plan in place with Illinois. The Dakotas and Western Iowa don't seem to be taking this seriously. Downstate Michigan is also problematic."

Chapter Nine

Klinger sighed. "You're right. They act as if this will be a temporary blip. Well, do what you can. We're warning the regional coordinators that they will probably face resistance from the bordering regions neighbors if they run into trouble through lack of planning. Remember, 'good fences make good neighbors'."

Jay said, "Point taken. Okay, let's run through the categories. First is housing. We have five factories up and running. All the prefabs we estimated will be ready and warehoused. We could even supply some of the other regions, if they ask. We will have both wood and metal prefabs.

"Second category is greenhouses. We will exceed plan in this area for structures. Where we will fall short is in soil and plants to finish their prep. I've attached our remediation plan."

Klinger said, "I do appreciate that whenever you bring a problem, you have a suggested solution. Just be aware, Professor Friedman, that I know about the trick of inventing problems in order to sell an unneeded solution."

Jay said, "If you ever think any of these problems are invented, I'll be delighted to give you chapter and verse, Colonel. Third category is water supplies. We will have pipelines from the Great Lakes to all our planned housing and industrial sites ready within two years. We have also predrilled a number of deep aquifer wells as a backup. Treatment plants and sewage handling are also running at or near schedule.

"Fourth category is power generation. Our renewables are in place. We are concerned about a contingency plan, particularly if post-event weather is problematic."

Klinger raised a hand and almost smiled. "Great news there. The Council has decided to put a nuclear power plant in your area. If you get any push back by people worried about byproducts, this is one of the next generation reactors. The plant will have a fuel supply on site sufficient to power your region for a projected twenty-five years. You need to start considering where to locate it. Let me transfer the specs to your cyberpad."

Jay said, "I'll reserve judgment until my advisors review safety and distribution plans. Nuclear plans still make me leery. But I'm old fashioned."

My next category is health care. Given the stress on the care system, we've invested significant moneys into the new autodoc systems. Their AIs have proven capable of extending the workforce almost fivefold in capability.

"Sixth category is transportation. Because of the uncertain conditions post-Event, we have invested heavily in blimps, dirigibles, and ultralights. Those plants will start coming on line by 2068.

"Finally category is public safety. We will have militia training camps available in adequate time. We can't start enrolling trainees until we can divulge the reason for the expanded need."

Colonel Klinger said, "Excellent overview, Doctor Friedman. Let's tear through the details before dinner, shall we."

Chapter Nine

CHAPTER TEN

15 May 2065

Madison, WI, USA

Ainsley and Addison were intent on celebrating. Their third semester as PhD candidates had been intense. The twins were used to racing through an academic landscape. They had begun high school two half years early. During their four years there, they completed over two years of university-accredited courses as well as the mandated curriculum. This enabled them to complete their bachelors' degrees in three jam-packed regular semesters plus summer courses. The PhD courses had been daunting.

Their apartment in Madison was more spartan than their Urbana digs had been. The twins missed the domestic touches that Rebecca and Sarah had added. Both had been far too busy to focus on decor. Fortunately, Rebecca and Sarah's rigorous housekeeping standards had stuck.

Ainsley disconnected the holovid call. "Aunt Cathy and Uncle Marty will definitely meet us at Aunt Karen's tomorrow for the cook-out. Cathy is bringing her famous bean salad and Uncle Marty has a supply of the pork chops from the hogs the tenants just butchered."

Addison said, "Good. I intend to sit on a lounge chair and make it earn its name." She sighed. Ainsley just nodded.

Over the last seventeen months, they had completed the bulk of the coursework required for their doctorates. It had been arduous. There had been times both women had considered taking a slower pace. However, both were eager to get beyond the theoretical. They had assimilated facts, figures, information, knowledge, and even bits of wisdom. They had absorbed analytic techniques and critical reasoning skills. They had a hunger to dedicate all this to the creation of something new and earth shaking. It was time to do research.

Chapter Ten

This weekend, though, was for relaxation. Addison said, "I confirmed dancing and fish fry with Cousin Jane and Aunt Karen for tonight. It's great we've finally become close with at least two of our Cameron relatives. Even though we've met several others as well, it saddens me that we still have never met our paternal grandparents." Ainsley thought, *Oh well, there's always next year. At least we can try to bridge a little of the family fissure. Tomorrow, Uncle Marty and Aunt Cathy will be joining us at the McFarland home of Karen and Jane.*

The meet-and-greet tomorrow would be either a time of healing or a continuation of decades of rancor. If it were simply a matter of logic, Ainsley and Addison were sure good will would prevail. However, Uncle Marty was Mommy's twin. Grandfather D's emphatic rejection had hurt Mommy badly. No one on the Cameron side had been willing to risk her Grandfather's wrath in all the long years since until Aunt Karen and Cousin Jane reached out. That bitter history would take the patience of a saint to forgive. Marty was no saint.

16 May 2065

McFarland, WI, USA

Everyone was on their best behavior. Aunt Karen was her usual, gentle, and welcoming, self. Cousin Jane was bouncing off the walls with repressed energy from completing her next-to-last undergraduate semester. Aunt Cathy had bonded with both immediately. Uncle Marty was slowly but inexorably thawing under the relentless bonhomie.

Then Aunt Karen started reminiscing about the Lost Years. She did this in all innocence. Addison and Ainsley had been avid listeners in the past when she gradually unwrapped the bandages around her memories. At first only Marty and Cathy got deathly still. Then everyone did. Karen blurted out, "I'm sorry Marty, Cathy. The four of us have danced around those awful years, as everybody does. Then Ainsley and Addison got me talking. Ultimately, it helped heal a lot of pain."

114

They all sat in silence for a moment. Then Marty began speaking in a monotone. "My journey of lost innocence began when Jihadis took Pop prisoner. I was young, scared, and vulnerable. Understandably, Mom was wrapped up in her own fears. She spent every moment organizing people to support Pop, trying to free him, or praying. My grandfather, Alex, came to live with us and was my constant companion.

"Papa Alex was seventeen when terrorist brought war to America in 2001. He enlisted as soon as he was eligible and fought in Afghanistan and Iraq. He was proud of defending his country. It was the high point of his life. He had passed those values down to Pop. While Pop was being tortured, Papa passed those values down to me.

"Years later, I would hear Pop and Papa arguing about the great American war machine, as Pop called it. Papa would begrudgingly agree that the Pentagon pricks had mismanaged things. 'If only they had left the Special Forces in charge, Afghanistan wouldn't have turned into a witches' cauldron.

"That was as far as he would go, though. He wouldn't agree jingoists and oil barons had stirred up the Iraq invasion. He truly thought we could and should have brought 'the American Way of Life' to the benighted tribesmen of the Middle East. He couldn't see these escapades were destroying that very way of life here; destroying our social compact and shared civic values."

Marty had his head lowered for a moment. First, Cathy put a hand on his. Then Jane did the same.

Jane began talking in the same low tones. "Our dad was the same way. Flew the flag every day. A life of service was a life worth living. My choice of service wasn't the military. Father was disillusioned with the Pentagon and passed that along to us. I did four tours with Doctors Without Borders. I was in Chad in '51, Myanmar/Burma in '52, back to Chad in '53, and in Sonora Mexico in '54."

Both sat in silent communion for a moment. They hadn't served together or served in the same way, but both had 'been there and done that.'

Marty finally nodded. "All right Addison and Ainsley. I know you have a million questions. I'll answer when I can. Bear with me when I can't."

The next day

Near Beijing, China

Daiyu was getting angry. This was an unusual accomplishment for her husband, Jian. Daiyu had the patience of a glacier. However, she had heard this same refrain from Jian for nearly a year now. She had hoped this evening dining out would be peaceful.

"Xiang should return now. First, we could use his skills and experience in the Pacification Planning Task Force. The boy has mastered many feats in bioengineering. China can benefit from its investment in him.

"Secondly, we have no firm predictions about when the collapse will come. Yes, the scientists say it will be a minimum of four to twelve years, but they seem to revise that every few months. If things deteriorate while he is in the United States, Xiang will be unable to rejoin us for years, if not decades. Who knows how a foreigner will fare in the US during frantic times?"

Daiyu took a deep breath and held it for ten seconds, counting slowly. Then she exhaled, equally slowly. "Our son is safe where he is. The turmoil that we will face in this nation will threaten everyone.

"Second, Xiang has more than paid any debt he might owe to the People's Republic. He is on full scholarship. He did years of youth service. Admit it, Jian. You want him back because you are finding it difficult to browbeat scientists to produce experimental results on a predictable schedule. You know it doesn't work that way and you would only end up alienating Xiang." She carefully didn't add, *Alienate him even more than you already have.*

The servers brought the first course of dim sum. The fragrances were lovely: with tinges of ginger, saffron, and soy.

She continued, switching to a less contentious topic. "What progress has our cyber experts made in developing AIs that can bring down the enemy's systems?"

Jian perked up. His attitude about cybernetics had shifted dramatically as the Long March North Program progressed. "If things continue at the same pace, we may achieve all our first phase goals with virtually no bloodshed. Once the first phase is completed, this will greatly hamper our enemy in any attempt at retaliation since our people will be intermingled with their own.

"However, our analysis shows a significant threat from the enemy's Advanced Studies Institute. They have the world's best bioengineers there. Our estimate is that this group potentially could put a corps of supersoldiers into the field in a few weeks. This is another reason we should bring Xiang home."

Daiyu put her head into her hands. The man was like one of those old time internet gifs from her childhood. The video would play for a short time and then, rerun from the beginning, endlessly.

She tried again, "Have you tried using your AIs for consultation on this? I understand they are diverse in their interests and abilities?"

Jian responded, "Our main AI, Cerberus, is focused, almost to the point of being narrow minded. The auxiliary has proven more flexible. It ran the factory district in Taipei. Its twin still does, with it as a backup." A thought struck him and his eyes got distracted. "Perhaps that is a key difference. It was in constant communication with several AIs, both its twin and an AI in Africa. I'll have the researchers look into that aspect."

Daiyu said, "Does your auxiliary AI have a name. I get confused when you vaguely refer to the thing as 'it'."

Jian barked a laugh. "It has the awkward name of ' Master Processor One of Two. If this research proves out and we give it primary responsibility, I will shorten its name to be 'The Master'.

Then there is a third AI we may be able to obtain from the United States. Thank you, Daiyu. As usual, your insights and fresh perspective have proven to be a treasure."

Daiyu thought, *Just when he is most exasperating, he can switch back to the man I love.*

1 June 2065

Madison, WI, USA

A ddison had worked into the wee hours at the cybercenter on her research project, Ainsley put in a holovid call to check on her sister. After a minute, Addison was checking on her. Ainsley pinched herself to become more alert *Addie can be intense.*

Ainsley said, "I am feeling far more anxiety than normal. I knew the Bioengineering Department was experiencing growing pangs, but I was surprised to learn that my primary advisor for my thesis research was to be another PhD candidate, Xu Xiang."

Addison interrupted. "Yeah. He was the cute sweeper, right?"

Ainsley said, "Yes, and a fine bioengineer, which is more relevant this morning Addie. I've heard that other universities, notably Cambridge-Oxford, tried this approach successfully. However, I relished the working relationship I established with Doctor Gunderson.

"I guess, when I am being honest with myself, I knew that the chair of a rapidly expanding department wasn't going to have spare cycles to devote to supervising my investigations. That is one of the key perquisites. Gunny waxes eloquent about his vineyards when we meet. The genetics of grapes is his focus. This allowed me free rein in the pursuit of my own interests."

Addison said, "Okay, but you and I both agreed we are – not immature, but inexperienced. We do need guidance."

Ainsley said, "I have no objections to Xiang, per se. The man is a brilliant scientist and about to publish a groundbreaking dissertation on his research. You're right. It's a bonus that he is an excellent sweeper on the intramural, co-ed soccer team where we're wings. It also doesn't hurt that he's cute, although that could be an issue for a professional relationship. A lot is riding on today's meeting."

Addison said, "I'm glad I'm not having the same complications in my research in the Cybernetics Department. My adviser, Doctor Shlomo Cohen, is brilliant as well. However, he's ancient, over fifty. If he ever played sports, it was decades ago. Finally, he's warm and gentle, but he definitely won't tempt me towards thoughts of an unprofessional liaison. You need to meet him, LeeLee. Hey, I gotta go."

◆◆◆

Ainsley walked down the basement corridor of the Human Bioengineering Lab. She would become intimately acquainted with these corridors over the next two years, but she had seldom ventured down here before today. *At least the hallways here are brightly lit and colorfully painted. The upstairs passages are drab, institutional gray tunnels. I wonder why?*

The sign on Xiang's lab entry was displaying a 'Come In' message. When Ainsley opened the door, she was amazed at the number and variety of cybernetics devices. *Did I wander into Addison's labs by mistake? I knew Xiang was working on border areas. That's why they thought some of my research ideas would resonate with his. Nevertheless, I expected to see more living organisms.*

Xiang called from the other side of the room. He stood straight. He had been stooped over, working on a piece of equipment. Ainsley was relieved to see there was a hog connected to the equipment. *Good. He's not only using lab animals, they are ones I have a high degree of familiarity with. Thanks Pop, Makes sense. Pigs are more intelligent than most think. Their physiology is similar to humans in many ways.*

Xiang was beaming as he advanced to shake Ainsley's hand. "Welcome Ms. Cameron. You're right on time. If you don't mind, we'll do a short tour of the facility and then talk over lunch. It's my treat. This morning I got word that the committee accepted my

119

dissertation. I only need to complete human studies. If those hold up, I should be Doctor Xu soon."

Ainsley said, "Congratulations. I can't wait to read the paper, if I'm allowed, that is."

Xiang said, "Certainly. If we are going to work together, we need to know how each other thinks. Let's start with..."

Xiang was starting on his third helping of Creole fritters, the house specialty of the Blue Bayou. Ainsley wasn't far behind with her second helping, but she believed she would have to cede the win to Xiang today. She sipped her ale, enjoying the contrast of the biting hops and the spicy seafood perfection.

Ainsley had never been to the Louisiana swamps, but the food here tempted her to brave the humidity, mosquitos, and gators. A stuffed gator hung precariously over Xiang's head. She even enjoyed the zydeco tunes, though they weren't at all like her usual technoscream.

Xiang wiped his lips and took a break. He sighed, "We Chinese believe our regional cuisines capture every possible culinary delight. However, whenever one of my compatriots starts belittling American blandness, I bring them here.

"Before I dig back in, let me ask you to tell me more about this MindMeld concept of yours. Pardon me, you were finished eating, weren't you?"

Ainsley pushed back from the table. "Yes, thank you, Xiang. Thank you for lunch and thank you for introducing me to the Blue. These truly are addicting.

"I have to give Addison credit for the initial project concept. Back at the U of I they were pushing us to declare majors. Addie and I had made a pact to choose different ones. That proved difficult since we do have similar interests and minds. Anyway, I settled on our field and she chose cybernetics later that evening.

"While she was contemplating our new fields, she started musing about the interfaces; the boundaries where the two sciences meet.

Serendipitously she also remembered another pair of twins we met who seemed to be able to read each other's minds. People thought we should be able to as well. Hence, MindMeld."

Xiang said, "I understand. Family connections often drive these career decisions. The reason I got into this field instead of cybernetics is that sad, old tale. I have a domineering father who belittles 'computers', as he sometimes calls them. He can see ways I'll be useful to him as a human bioengineer. He doesn't stop to think about what I want. My Mother doesn't resist him directly, but I'm too impatient to resist passively as she does.

"Is your family story similar Ainsley?"

Ainsley quietly said, "My parents and younger brother were murdered three years ago."

Xiang was aghast. "Please forgive my clumsiness. I had no idea."

Ainsley said, "It's not your fault Xiang. We don't talk about it if we don't have to."

Xiang gently took one of her hands in his. His warm touch penetrated the ice-cold lump Ainsley had felt growing in her breast.

◆◆◆

As they walked back from lunch, Ainsley asked Xiang, "Would you please give me an overview of your dissertation topic and findings?"

Xiang smiled again at the memory of the committee's acceptance of his work. "Modern human bioengineering techniques generally fall into two major categories. The first is prosthetics. Any artificial construct intended to replace or extend a normal human function is essentially a form of prosthetic.

"The other major category is any biologically-based enhancement. Researchers base most of these in manipulation of the individual's DNA. We're beginning to use a subset of these techniques to change inheritable characteristics for the next generation.

"Some techniques span both categories. The science is a spectrum with two nodal peaks. My work lies in the interface."

Chapter Ten

The colleagues paused at a busy street corner, waiting for the light to change. They watched the speeding bicyclists most carefully. They were more of a risk than the hovercars guided by AIs.

Once across the street, Xiang continued. "The problem I decided to tackle was behavioral issues. This would include those problems that society used to call 'mental illness', as well as other behavioral patterns people might wish to modify – addictive behaviors, overeating, and certain modalities of expressing oneself. The list is virtually endless.

"This area has stymied science for at least a century and a half. The underlying systems are complex, with a huge number of interacting components. However, we have begun to develop precision diagnostic tools. We have identified a reasonable number of intervention points. My work explores ways to exploit this new knowledge. We're building a tool chest that will address a plethora of problems in standardized ways. This includes some gene mods, implanted stimulators, individually crafted pharma, and others.

"One set of tools I have yet to test thus far is an extension of talk therapy. Historically, talk therapy has been effective for some problems, particularly in combination with pharma. The biggest issue is that personal crisis points seldom coincide with scheduled counseling sessions."

Ainsley was fascinated. This was a vast area of study. The limitation of her own research vision humbled her. She asked, "What technique do you envision to address that?"

Xiang said, "Swarms of nanobots controlled by artificial intelligence. Their first responsibility will be to identify the crisis point. Once they diagnose the need, they start multi-tasking. First, they notify the individual's caregivers of the situation. Second, if the patient has any pharma-dispensing implants embedded in their body, the 'bots trigger their use. Third, the 'bots start a whispered conversation with the patient, delivering standardized talk therapy until a licensed practitioner can relieve them."

There was a bench in a shady nook beside the Human Bioengineering Building. Xiang guided Ainsley there. She had been thinking about this last revelation. She had a mental itch and needed to scratch it.

"Pardon Me Xiang. Or since this is a professional conversation, possibly I should day Doctor Xu."

Xiang waved that away. "No, it will always be Xiang for you Ainsley."

Touched, she said, "Then please, call me LeeLee. That's my friends' name for me.

"I have a concern about behavior modification in general, but particularly this last technique. It would seem to lend itself easily to abuse. I can see an authoritarian government using vast swarms of these nanobots to turn their entire population into subservient, unthinking slaves."

Xiang said, "I understand your concern. Both our past governments have histories of this kind of action. Ultimately, the human spirit won out in each case, but the toll was high.

"Every technology has the potential of being abused. Malicious actors could twist even your seemingly innocuous MindMeld in the same way you envision the powerful misusing my 'bots. This will be a wonderful topic to consider. Please draft up an outline. I propose we work on it together. If we can design concrete safeguards, I propose joint publication in the journals."

This is wonderful. Xiang is treating me like a colleague, an equal. This is the beginning of a wonderful relationship.

Xian said, "Oh, before I forget. Now that you are spending less time on classroom work, the school will want you to begin mentoring one or two beginning PhD candidates. We will start with introductions and casual conversations until they get to the same stage you've achieved. If you're interested, I have a woman who I think will be a good match."

Ainsley said, "I understand. It's a little flattering, as well as daunting, to think of myself in that role."

Chapter Ten

Xiang laughed. "You should have heard my self-talk when I had to meet you for the first time. Salutatorian at age sixteen. I was delighted to find out you were a warm and friendly, down-to-earth person.

"If you agree, I can introduce you to Yasmeen tomorrow morning. Her name is Yasmeen Khan. She's from the Kashmir state of India (although Pakistan still formally claims it as well). She reminds me of you in a way. She intends to work on her degree throughout summers and breaks. She is in a hurry to make her mark on the world. Naturally, since she is in our program, she is a world-class academic.

"At this point, she is more conservative in her approach. I believe her devout Muslim faith deters her from considering any alterations to individual's DNA. We will respect her beliefs, but we will see if there is any latitude for her to consider more than prosthetics. If you have time, you might want to consult the imam at the Islamic Students Center for insight and advice."

Ainsley and Xiang halted at the foot of the stairs into the lab. Ainsley would depart once their talk ended.

Ainsley said, "I come from a strong, conservative religious tradition as well. My mother's family are staunch Roman Catholics. My father converted when he proposed. It caused a bitter rift, which persists until today. That's another point on which Yasmeen and I can connect."

Xiang said, Are you deeply religious then, Ainsley?"

She said, "No Xiang. I'm struggling now. When our family was murdered, I went through all the classic stages. I should say I cycled through them multiple times. I felt shock, denial, anger, bargaining, guilt, and depression. Hope has eluded me. At first, I directed my anger solely at the perpetrators. Then I got angry with God, which made me doubt the God the Church taught me about could exist.

"I'm still searching for answers at this stage. My sister talked to me about the evolution of God or goodness in the world. A theologian called it ' consciousness becoming'. That's the closest I come at the moment."

CHAPTER ELEVEN

14 June 2065,

Milwaukee, WI., USA

The family would usually be in church by this time on a Sunday morning. Hope would be there because of her responsibilities as the choir director. *Grand-mère* would be there to get ready to meet her Maker; the one she expected to see any day. Mama would be there to have some quiet time before all the neighborhood gossips started chatting with her. She needed to pray for her Joe. Aunt Ceci would be there to maintain her extended web of connections that kept them all safe in a dangerous city. Cousin Jacqueline would be there because she couldn't stand being alone with herself, even now, two and a half years after her world shattered.

Today instead, the Scott family was huddled in front of their cheap little holographic video projector. The news was running a constant recital of the gruesome statistics along with bits of videos of the explosion captured by distant security cameras. The tragic events even engaged Jacqueline, who was murmuring "How horrible," again and again.

Hope thought, *Good. This is the first time she's getting out of thinking only of herself. I still have nightmares and such from Uncle Robert's attack. Queenie suffered for over a year. I wish Ceci hadn't taken her out of school, but the counselor agreed and thought it was best.*

The disaster mesmerized all of them. Hope said, "It reminds me of the neighborhood crowds who gather near a collapsed building still smoldering from a drug lab explosion. That's become such a familiar scene in our neighborhoods over the last few months."

Aunt Ceci said, "They say it's because foreign supplies have disappeared. But why would anyone do this horrible thing?"

There weren't any local crowds viewing the explosion in Berlin. News choppers were only beginning to arrive in the area from

126

surrounding cities. They kept their distance. The newscasters explained, "Partly that is to avoid damage and contamination from the huge storm of debris. Partly that is to enable our international viewers to see the signature mushroom-shaped cloud. For the benefit of youngsters who hadn't seen history vids of the nuking of two Japanese cities and the use of a tactical nuke in Afghanistan, we'll show those now. Our science commentators will be explaining the significance of the cloud shape."

Abruptly, *Grand-mère* lifted her bulky frame from her recliner. "Come, *mes enfants*, we need to go pray for all these lost souls. Hope will need to choose different hymns for today as well. We are doing nothing of use sitting here."

Aunt Ceci started passing out the guns to each person. Only *Grand-mère* refused, once again. She always said, "If the hoodlums want my life, then my Savior will welcome me that much sooner. As trembling as my hands are, I would hurt one of my beloved family."

As the last person left their apartment, Aunt Ceci armed the defense systems and turned on the bright warning sign. They didn't want any potential invaders to miss the notice. Twice now, they had needed to clean up and dispose of bodies. The neighborhood watch group helped. After the insanity of dealing with the police after Joe and Robert killed each other, all knew the officials were of no help at all.

They walked the five blocks to their storefront church, everyone's eyes were constantly moving. They gave everyone a careful scan, even known people like Jimmy, the tostadas street vendor. Drugs could render anyone dangerous. The homemade junk hitting the streets lately was especially lethal.

Aunt Ceci had equipped everyone with tactical headgear from the black market. That way, all could easily talk though they had dispersed for safety. Mama said, "All this rising violence. It reminds me of the worst days of the Lost Years. What did the Reverend call it now? The Times of Trouble.

Chapter Eleven

"I thought all this was behind us until last year. Then, there was that revolution in Italy. They tried to make it sound like a minor thing, calling it the Italian Dustup. Mrs. Cavliano – you know, the grocer's mother – told me that over three million people died. Dustup indeed!"

Aunt Ceci usually didn't say much, focusing on assessing threats instead. This time, she replied. "I think when we have stable times, like the last ten years, people get lured into wishfully thinking those are normal. They forget what the Good Book says. 'Through many tribulations we must enter the kingdom of God.' Watch out on your right Jacqueline."

The last block took them right past Charlie's new hangout. As usual, he had a throng of young children flitting about. The would-be gangsters did much of Charlie's dirty work; distributing drugs, running numbers, enforcing the gang rules with knives and improvised weapons. Guns were scarce now. The police could scan for them from fifty meters. Any illegal guns were justification for immediate use of lethal force. The state had licensed all the Scott family's weapons and supplied them with embedded id chips.

Hope wished there was another route to church. If there were, Charlie would lie in wait there. He had tried every ploy he could to coerce Hope to 'dance' in his clubs. He became especially bold after the video of her rape went viral. She had quickly disabused him of the idea he could blackmail her. Everyone in the community already knew all the details anyway.

Mama had summarized it pithily. "The threat of sexual violence sticks to him like stink sticks to a skunk." Aunt Ceci never said anything, but Hope noted that her gun never wavered from its aim at Charlie's center mass whenever he was in range.

Same day,

Paris, France

Rahel Blumstein couldn't move. She was still on the hyperloop train from Berlin to Paris. Word began to spread of the calamity. *I'm relieved that my trip had spared me, but*

128

most of my family and friends must have perished. The worst is that I convinced many of them to leave Israel and Palestine and flee to Berlin, all in the name of safety. The guilt had made her vomit twice already. Now she had no one to share her misery with.

The man in a seat across the aisle from her had an internet news site open. There was an unconfirmed report that a malfunctioning robot had triggered the bomb. The only question was whether the robotic mechanisms had failed or if the controlling artificial intelligence was at fault.

This news snapped Rahel out of her self-flagellation. *What was it David Levi, the founder of the new splinter group, named The Collective told me?*

It came to her. David had said. "The work of Abrahams' Children is good. They are making some progress in bridging sectarian differences between Christians, Muslims, and Jews. However, the real threat now isn't coming from humans and our differences. The machines and the warped ones who call themselves enhanced people are worse enemies."

Rahel had been dismissive at the time. Now she had a mission and a leader.

Next day,

Moscow, Russia

Svetlana Tereshkova was venting her frustrations in a talk with her mother. She pushed her glasses back up her nose. "The Institute refused to consider my proposal to build a space elevator. The spectacular failure of the multinational effort in the Pacific provided ample ammunition for the naysayers. They are afraid to take risks."

Her mother dusted the flour off her apron and said, "People did die there Lanachik." She put the bread in the oven to proof.

Svetlana had carefully marshalled all her arguments. "The Brazilian-led team rushed their deployment in a greedy effort to corner a market. Russia materials science has made great strides forward, particularly in comparison to the conglomerate's suppliers.

"The original effort did done one thing correctly. They funded another speculative company to shepherd asteroids into the vicinity of Earth. Nearly a hundred asteroids now sail near the Earth and the Moon. Solar sails powered them. Thereby, they can continue their graceful pirouettes for centuries, guided by onboard AIs with no danger of collisions or mishaps. This cuts down the cost for a Russian elevator tremendously.

"Next, a Russian scientist is the one who developed the original concept. It would be a betrayal of our history and culture not to lead the glorious fulfillment of this dream. The Americans and Chinese have efforts underway to deploy space elevators at Quito, Mount Talakmau in Indonesia, and in Kenya. The window of opportunity is narrowing."

Her mother asked, "Did the appeal to patriotism move him?"

Svetlana said, "The head of the Institute almost patted me on her head and told me to go play with my construction set. At least, that was the way I interpreted his patronizing tone. 'Russia sits far from the Equator, where these contrivances must be built. Let others pay the price of testing out all the hundreds of failure points first.' If my face wasn't so plain, I would have tried flirting with him."

Her mother had tsked. "He obviously doesn't know you. Your beauty and fierce will are hidden from idiots. Now that you're mad, he better watch his back." She smiled.

Svetlana appreciated her mother's constancy. However, her average looking face and body combined with her technical focus led many men dismiss her out of hand.

Svetlana said, "At least one person on the panel was supportive. Yuri Morizov is a rising star at the Bureau of Resource Planning. He's the driving force pushing deployment of Russia's hyperloop network. Word is that he wants to connect 'loops internationally and even used advanced materials science to construct transoceanic 'loops.

"Yuri approached me about transferring my efforts to his team. The requirements for transoceanic tubes that can safely convey a massive hyperloop vactrain would stretch the capabilities of the team and me.

"I pledged to work with Yuri and support his efforts, but I'm still committed to reaching the stars in a way that will be environmentally responsible and sustainable. A space elevator uses virtually no fuel to get something to near earth orbit."

10 February 2066

La Paz, Bolivia

The march of chaos continued around the world. The various overlords of humanity focused on self-preservation and accumulation of survival goods rather than preservation of social order.

Jose Quintana was the kingpin of a small cartel group. The short, wiry man was discussing the situation with his chief chemist, Emilio, at their city offices. "We criminals noticed the change first. Not just those of us in the pharmaceuticals trade. Corporate criminals, political criminals, and organized syndicates began exploiting the situation almost immediately, as a reflex action. However, the criminal class is predominantly conservative in nature. They prefer their environment to be stable, predictable."

Emilio peered blindly through his coke-bottle-thick glasses. "Of course. If we don't know what our markets and competition are likely to do, we risk vast sums of money."

Jose continued. "As the reins of law and order continued to loosen, the criminal aristocracy is becoming nervous. They ordered their analysts to discover the root causes. While the lowest level criminals ran riot, doubling and redoubling crime statistics, the analysts dug until they uncovered the conspiracy of silence the top-level political leaders had entered into."

This perked up Emilio's interest. "What did they discover?" He sipped from his coffee mug.

Jose said, "There is a world-wide catastrophe coming soon. Once the syndicate leaders and cartel bosses understood the situation they faced, they tended to react in either one of two ways. Many decided to emulate the oligarchs who were part of the conspiracy from the beginning. Those cowards have liquidated assets as quickly and quietly as possible. They hired top-notch consultants to advise them on how to preserve their personal assets – and the leaders' lives.

"The minority of the rest of us reacted the same way a small minority of the highest political leaders did. We see a power vacuum. Nature and ambitious people abhor vacuums. This is a golden opportunity Emilio. We will end up controlling entire countries."

The meeting occurring in La Paz, Bolivia was identical, in spirit, to countless gatherings in rooms around the world during the years between 2063 and 2067. The faceless people here were the most powerful men in the region other than a handful of generals. The speaker now was Quintana.

"Si, I understand the projections of the scientists who say the crisis will be in three to ten years. My offer still stands to any who are willing. I will buy you out. You take your money, jewels, and other assets. Any of your security forces who choose to can accompany you and take their weapons. I will buy the rest for ten cents on the dollar. No one else will make a better offer."

It was obvious the others thought him a fool. Quintana calculated that the Andes were as safe as anywhere else was on Earth. Yes, the market for their product and all their distribution sources was collapsing. Quintana was still willing to roll the dice. Something would come up if he controlled the region.

9 April 2066

London, Kingdom of England and Wales

132

Scotland Yard hadn't seen this level of unrest since the last secession vote had removed Northern Island from (the former) Great Britain. Things had begun to sort themselves out. However, the last few months had seen crazies coming out of the woodwork.

Sergeant Heartwood was kitted out in regulation uniform instead of her usual casual attire of jumper and the newly fashionable culottes. The uniform was stiff from disuse and chafed at all the most sensitive points. The full body armor under the jumper and skirt was a comfort, however unflattering it was to the vain woman.

She turned to her inspector. "What's the drill today Mary? Is it more of the Ultra Greens fighting the Southsiders?"

Mary said, "I'm not sure Janet. I know the tactical squads forming up in the football stadium since the Powers that Be have seen Dire Things in their crystal balls. I hope they are as far off the mark as they were last week." The inspector was checking the charges for her stun gun and giving her plastic shield a quick wipe.

The sergeant's amplifying ear buds picked up the sounds of a crowd approaching. She notified her inspector with a wave and cued up a surveillance camera from around the corner. She zoomed in on the posters the lead marchers were carrying. Her inspector joined her.

The inspector flicked a stray set of bangs back up under her helmet. "Lord help us. That one sign says, 'The Icecaps Are Melting'. The next says, 'Prepair to Drown'. Ignorant git. Greenland and the poles have ice sheets for which one should 'prepare', unless their suggesting we get a partner before the collapse.

"It's Ultra Greens then. My cousin in Australia fought in pitched battles against the likes of these. Vicious brutes he said."

She turned to the other squad. "Deploy the mobile barrier across India Dock please. We'll try to route them in a loop back onto themselves. That might take the piss out of them."

Chapter Eleven

They stood tensely for a moment. The momentum of the crowd seemed to have slowed as they rounded the curve and saw the police barricades. All the police hoped the demonstrators would take a deep breath and remain peaceful.

The sergeant felt a pinch under her left arm and twisted to relieve the irritation. Because of that, she saw the five people equipped with some sort of jetpack hopping off the rooftops behind them. She screamed an alert and keyed the 'officer needs assistance' button on her utility belt. Half her compatriots reacted in time and reversed their shields. The other half fell like tenpins.

Same day,

Madison, WI, USA

Lilly, one of the lab techs, looked up, white-faced. "Yasmeen, didn't you say you have a cousin who works in London?"

Yasmeen swept her long, black tresses into a hand and tucked it back under headscarf. She had been viewing a sample under a microscope and looked preoccupied when she lifted her head. "I'm sorry, Lilly. What did you say?"

Lilly had tears in her eyes. "There's bad news from London. Where does your cousin work in the City?"

Yasmeen was laser-focused now. She said quietly, Farah works in the Canary Wharf financial and trading district. Why? What's the news?"

Lilly half-sobbed. "There's fighting at Canary Wharf. The reports say dozens of police officers were killed and hundreds of civilians. Buildings are on fire and they show an ongoing battle. The news crews are being shot at as well. Naturally, the reporting is confused."

Yasmeen had her cyberpad out. She had to look up Farah's coordinates. Her first cousin and she had been like two peas in a pod growing up. People often thought they were sisters with their caramel complexions, raven locks, and long, athletic builds.

However, Farah and she had gone separate ways after their undergraduate days. Farah had become involved in international

134

affairs, working at the Stockholm Climate Conference. After that, Yasmeen's father, the Shah, had hired Farah to handle his international affairs in London.

Farah's holographic video finally popped up. She was on a sunny beach. Yasmeen gave a deep sigh as Farah said, "Hi Meeni-ji. What's the occasion?"

◆◆◆

Yasmeen found it hard to return her assays. She was relieved Farah was safe on holidays in the Canary Islands rather than at the Canary Wharf battle zone. Odd conjunction of vacation location and workplace names. *Wonder if Rah-Rah did that on purpose. She was certainly shocked when I told her about the riots. We watched the reports together for a few minutes then she said she had to call friends from the office.*

Yasmeen received quiet murmurs of support from the workers around her. These personal interactions sensitized her. When Ainsley Cameron, one of her graduate student peer advisors came into the lab a few minutes later, Yasmeen immediately zeroed in on Ainsley's unusual behavior.

Yasmeen walked over and sat beside Ainsley. *She definitely isn't her normal cheery self. I know she knows I'm here. I'll sit and wait a moment. If she wants to talk, she will.*

A tear leaked out of the corner of Ainsley's eye. Yasmeen said nothing. She put an arm around the other woman and pulled a small square of cloth from her sleeve. Ainsley whispered, "Thanks. Can we get some coffee?"

The two women left the basement and took the stairs to the second floor break room. Once they each had their drink they went outside to a bench. The icy wind off Lake Mendota was bone chilling until they reached the sheltered, sunny nook.

Ainsley spoke in such a low voice that Yasmeen had difficulty hearing her at first. "Seemed like such a nice guy. Can't believe I was that stupid. Let him con me up to his room for the wallet he 'forgot'. Caught me unaware and overpowered me. When done, he told me he had a holovid of the whole thing. Unless I wanted it put on the internet, I'd come back tomorrow for 'another round'.

"That's when he found out I was a state champion soccer (you call it football) striker. I shot for the far corner post and he dropped to the floor, gasping. He also didn't know I nearly became a cybernetics major. Didn't take me a minute to find his equipment, wipe all his drives, and disable the whole setup.

"He was starting to get up, facing away from me. I did a penalty kick shot. Then I warned him he needed to drop out of school and leave Madison. Otherwise, he'd find out how I helped my grandfather castrate the other type of pigs. I have a feeling he believed me by that point."

Yasmeen said, "Do you want to report it to the police? Did you go to Uni Hospital to be checked out?"

Ainsley said, "No. Wouldn't do any good to go to the police. My cousin warned me, 'If you can't prove he used force or used a weapon, they won't even bother to question him.'

"As for the medical question, I have the equivalent of a medical degree in training and experience. Our lab downstairs had all the supplies I needed. I'll be fine."

Yasmeen waited for several more heartbeats. Then she said, "You've been a wonderful mentor to me Ainsley. I'd like to return the favor if I may. For what it's worth, I strongly suggest you get counseling. You could talk to a rape counselor or to your spiritual advisor. Post-traumatic stress from this is almost inevitable. Second, I've trained in martial arts. It would be an honor and privilege if you would let me teach you. You can go for formal classes if you want. However, I believe taking that type of training, coupled with what you did to the beast, will help you heal your soul and return your sense of power."

Ainsley said, "Thanks Yasmeen. I'm going to do even more than that. I'm going to start a campaign to have every woman in the department trained in self-defense and rape prevention. I also have an idea how I can use bioengineering to give women extra protection. It will, at least, make men think twice before they force themselves on someone they think isn't able to fight back."

13 November 2067

Milwaukee, WI, USA

Aunt Ceci called a family conference. "There's no way to soften this. I just got a message from my banker, Fernando. There's been a bank crash and a run. My savings were mostly wiped out. I won't be able to pay the security services going forward.

"Because of that, I've bought extra guns and body armor for all of us. Y'all know the rate of sexual violence has gone through the roof everywhere. As a group of women, it'll be up to each of us to protect each other and ourselves.

"We have enough to get groceries for the next five months. We own the apartment and the taxes and utilities are also covered. However, we can't afford any extras. Queenie, no more rental vids. *Mère*, I'm sorry, no more pastries."

Everyone looked around the clean and comfortable apartment. This had been home for most of them for years. Where would they go?

Hope Scott was frightened. She said, "Charlie and others of his ilk will be circling the same way the wolves do around caribou in the NatGeo cinevids. I had to use my gun to stop three men who cornered me in midafternoon last week. It's only going to get worse." She and Ceci both looked at the young Jacqueline. She was barely recovering from the trauma of her father's repeatedly raping her. She wouldn't survive another assault.

20 November 2067

Milwaukee, WI, USA

"Mama, Ceci, I've heard about a new defense for women to combat sexual violence. It takes a few weeks I want to take Jacqueline with me to Northern Wisconsin. I want you, *Grand-mère*, and Ceci to go to Madison while we're there. I have friends from college doing graduate work there. You can stay with them for a few weeks. I'll tell Jacqueline you're checking out colleges for her for next year. She is so far removed from practical reality; she won't question that. Nor will *Grand-mère.*"

Ceci said, "Madison's dangerous too, but it is better than Milwaukee. I've submitted the paperwork. Everyone can take their guns."

Mama asked, "What is this new defense called Hope?"

Hope said, "It's called the Clipper Mama. That's all I can tell you now."

Oh The Humanity

CHAPTER TWELVE

7 November 2067

Austin, TX., USA

"Hi Javier. What's your take on the war between China and Russia? Guess it's not the little brushfire spat the colonel portrayed last week." The R.O.T.C. cadets were gathering in an assembly room near their drill field.

Javier was a tall, muscular Hispanic. He brushed his new mustache and tugged his R.O.T.C. cadet's uniform into a neat trim. "Hey Rich. No, it's definitely much more. The briefing will give us the details, but my sources say China has poured the People's Liberation Army and millions of other people across the border. It looks like they intend to stay. This is the most serious geopolitical situation this century."

Rich was fifteen centimeters shorter than Javier, red-haired, and pale skinned. He shook his head. "What can they be thinking? Why invade Siberia? This makes no sense to me."

Javier's jaw was tight, teeth clenched. "That worries me too. What worries me more is that these things have a history of spinning out of control. I think the decreasing isolationism of the USA is good overall, but there's a danger that goes with it. Here comes the colonel. Attention."

The gray-haired colonel and mechanical engineering professor strode into the crowded, bright-lit room. "At ease. People, I'm sorry to have to tell y'all I'm mobilizing this unit as of today. I've notified the UT administration. They will inform all of your professors. If your duties allow and your professors agree, you may attempt to finish your courses remotely."

Javier took a deep breath. *Could the Siberian situation we were talking about be behind all this? Naw. Probably a drug ring needs reining in.*

The colonel brought up the image of their oath to the Constitution. "I need to remind y'all of your oaths. What I am about to reveal to you is covered by the Official Secrets Act, as amended Thursday 3rd November of this year, four days ago."

He took a deep breath. "People, the whole world has been hoodwinked for over five years. The Stockholm Protocols were window dressing to lull people into complacency. The truth is that climate change has reached a critical point. The current estimate is that the ice sheets in Greenland and Antarctica will collapse totally within the next six months." The cadets were quiet, but snapped to rigid attention automatically.

"The thawing of all the ice will raise the seal level sixty-six meters. If this happens, the impact on the USA, particularly its coastal areas will be the worst natural disaster imaginable.

"No, the ice is unlikely to collapse in one fell swoop. No, the ice won't all melt immediately. This means we have time to prepare our citizens, if they will believe us after all these years of fraud and deceit."

The student warriors began to buzz in consternation. The colonel rapped the desk behind him. "The civilian officials are giving us until the beginning of the year to prepare plans to achieve three major objectives. First, we are to preserve good order. Second, we are to develop evacuation plans for the entire coastal area. Third, we are to help prepare refugee camps.

"We won't be performing these tasks alone, nor necessarily be in the lead in any one of them. I spent the morning with a regional task force. We had representatives from the state and local authorities."

One of the cadets asked, "Colonel wasn't there anyone from the federal level? That's surprising."

The colonel barked out something between a laugh and a derisive expletive. "The regional director was a total waste of space. She's focusing on helping people like the energy industry. She doesn't even think about the hundreds of millions of lives at risk."

Javier was mystified. "Sir, the energy industry has almost totally left the Gulf Coast. Why would she waste any time on them?"

Chapter Twelve

The colonel rolled his shoulders. "She's been working to help them out for years. Why do you think all those companies moved to high ground; out of a benevolent desire to help the depressed Midwest?"

The cynical tone of the colonel shocked Javier, not that he blamed him. The longer he thought about it, the angrier he got. He turned to Rick and whispered. "I couldn't understand why they would hide this from us for five years. Now I get it. They had to feather their nests and fill their coffers before panic broke out."

The colonel continued, "There was one federal rep who was squared away. The Congressional Representative from Beaumont, Sam Houston Beauregard, looks like he will be a help. He knows how to shake the bureaucratic trees. Guess he hasn't caught the Beltline disease."

The next day,

Outside of Adelaide, Victoria,
Australia

The massive set of engines struggled to move the skyscraper up the incline into the hills northeast of the city. This was Adelaide's largest building. Darby heard a loud bang and immediately shut the apparatus down.

The wiry First Nations Person hopped out of the cab, cyberpad in one hand and the key to the tool chest in another. First, he carefully watched as the twenty-four mechanical legs of the building-moving platform lowered massive feet to support and stabilize the skyscraper. His team was moving the structure over fifty kilometers from the city center to its new home in the hills.

Darby trusted that the initial crews had stabilized and reinforced the roadbed and the area to each side to support the massive weight. However, he was personally responsible. He was going to verify that no local issue would threaten his perfect record. They were out in the middle of farmland here.

The weather was nice at least, cool for November. This part of the coastal area was largely agricultural. To Darby's unpracticed eye, it looked like most people had evacuated, but they could all just be working sheep over the next rise.

While the rest of his twenty-person crew and he stretched, took drinks of tea, and relieved themselves in the bush, Darby ran his programs through an automated check of the forty thousand plus sensors that the team had distributed throughout his equipment and plastered in the skyscraper. It would be wonderful if the noise were random, possibly a hunter discharging a weapon nearby. Everyone was supposed to remain at least ten kilometers away from the middle sections of the track. Nevertheless, sound travelled great distances here in the bush, he was overly sensitive and on edge, and his fellow citizens didn't always regard laws and regulations with the greatest of reverence.

His cyberpad's AI flashed an alert. "Harry, the dinkum-thinkum says engine number eleven is our problem child. It thinks it's a pinion that snapped."

The entire team groaned. This would be one of the most time-consuming problems possible, short of a collapse of the building. The designers had done as much as they could to allow components to be accessible and easy to service, but this was the worst-case scenario. They would need to remove the drivetrain of the engine to gain access. Fortunately, they had spare parts and assemblies for all the critical systems.

Darby checked the inventory. "Judith, there is a replacement drivetrain in bin thirty-two. Pull it please. Mary, get the slider pallets out please. Let's get cracking everyone. It's only going to get hotter. I want to get back in the cab in time for my beauty nap."

They all laughed. Harry called out, "You need one mate. Hope it works. I'm tired of looking at your ugly mug."

Darby called the control center at their Barossa Valley destination. "G'day Control. This is Team Three. We have a breakdown just past marker post forty-one. We have what we need. My estimate is repairs will take about two to three hours. I'll give you updates as we get further into it."

Chapter Twelve

"Thank you Team Three. We'll have the beer chilled when you get here."

"Thanks Team Three. How about a few bottles of Shiraz? Some of the team will want the beer, but I want to elevate their taste."

"Will do mate."

Darby heard a yelp from under the platform. He ran over. Mary called out. "There's a nest of jumping ants under here. Somebody bring me a bottle of spray."

The chief engineer, Emily Southfield, handed Darby a glass of wine when he entered the makeshift office. "It's not a whole bottle Darby, but it is good Shiraz. Cheers." The short, brown-haired woman clicked her glass against his.

After each took a sip, the chief engineer continued. "I've checked the records. You've completed the online course we outlined when I hired you Darby. I made a deal with you. Now, I want to offer you that position on my staff. Without a degree, I can't give you the full title of engineer. Officially, you're a trainee. However, the pay and responsibilities are as a full engineer. Congratulations Darby, you've earned it."

Darby looked out the window at the new skyline of Adelaide, rising here in the hills and felt a rising sense of pride and completion. The Shiraz was a little sweet for his taste, but a fitting celebratory drink.

The chief engineer said, "Your first task will be as the lead on the seawall design project. It has top priority and a tight, tight schedule. Preliminary design sketches are loading to your cyberpad now."

Darby's eyebrows wrinkled. "Why are we doing a seawall Chief? I thought the scientists calculated the maximum sea rise and we put the buildings above that level."

She said, "You're right. However, cyclones and tsunamis may well result from all the changes we'll experience soon. In truth, it will be multiple seawalls – three to be exact. That way we can have a

144

protected seaport against anything we can conceive of other than a deep-ocean meteor strike."

29 March 2068

Houston, TX., USA

Javier Gonzales didn't want to yell at his sister. After their parents and sister died in an auto accident, Angela dropped out of her successful band and took a job in a brokerage doing clerical work to support him through college. He owed her everything and he loved her.

He tried to keep his voice level and calm. "Angie, I don't care what your friends are telling you or what the news is saying. The flooding seven weeks ago isn't the end. Don't even think about coming back to our house in Pearland. That will be a deathtrap."

Angela was angry. "If it's that dangerous, what are you doing in Houston? This is bull Javier. We've sat in that house through category six hurricanes. Don't try to pull the handicapped card on me. I may be in a wheelchair, but my car could get me out if an emergency evacuation is called for in the end. The news channels all say this is overblown nonsense and the ocean will be subsiding soon. Why don't y'all work on restoring the internet? It's been over two months."

Javier bit off his words. "I'm doing my duty Angie. I'm trying to save the lives of fools... I'm sorry. . I'm trying to save the lives of people who won't listen to scientists instead of rabble-rousers. We have hovercopters to get out of town when the time comes. It will come Angie. That's why they pulled us out of school. That's why I can't see you this weekend.

"There's nothing I or anyone I know can do about the internet. The Chinese have a constant onslaught of attacks going on. It's part of their war against the Russians. Believe me; I'd fix it if I could.

"I'm begging you, Angie. Please stay in Austin. I'll try to see you in a few days. Frankly, we've already evacuated those who are willing to listen. The only real work we're doing now is preventing looting. They are keeping our vehicles fueled and have an observer plane flying out over the Gulf." Javier was operating on three hours of sleep and had to struggle to keep his tone mild.

Angie was still red in the face. She said, "Fine Javi. I'll stay here for another week. We'll talk when you visit." She disconnected.

Javier sighed and put his cyberpad into his backpack. The team's break was almost over. None of his squad was thrilled about patrolling deserted commercial districts with boarded up stores.

The news crews were the worst. All of them had an agenda, usually it was to try to make the National Guard and the cadets look like storm troopers. There hadn't been any incidents yet, although some of the reporters' equipment had been damaged – coincidentally when they wouldn't abide by orders.

1 April 2068

Houston, TX., USA

Javier was disoriented. He had fallen asleep barely an hour and a half before, as soon as they reached the tents in this city park. The previous day had been exhausting and depressing. Crowds of protestors and rowdies had confronted them throughout the day. After night fell, they found themselves in running battles with would-be looters. Then they had ended up firing on a crowd. Three of the crowd died, including an eleven-year old child. Javier was haunted.

"Get up Gonzales. We have five minutes to get to the choppers. Move!"

Javier threw on his uniform, autolaced his boots, and grabbed his pack. He double checked his area and found his cyberpad under the cot. He didn't remember taking it out last night. He did a quick run through of the toilets and headed outside.

He saluted the National Guard lieutenant. "I ran a check lieutenant. Barracks are cleared sir."

The lieutenant saluted. "Get aboard now cadet."

Javier buckled into the chopper. Once the lieutenant boarded, the hovercopter lifted off before he could find a seat. Javier turned to the woman to his left. "Do you know what's happening?"

She said, "The observation plane spotted a tsunami wave. We don't know how big it is, whether it will reach this far inland, or how soon until it hits. Orders are to get aloft and be ready to dump us out upland. The crews can come back for relief work."

Javier asked, "Will the swamp boats be ready for us to use?"

She said, "I don't know. I'll pass the question down to the lieutenant."

Someone said, "A tsunami can move as fast as a jet plane in deep water. Once it reaches shallows, it slows down to thirty to fifty kilometers per hour. Any vehicle can outpace it easily, if the roads are clear."

Javier said, "I don't think it'll be that easy. Have you ever seen a hurricane evacuation? They start those days in advance, and the roads are impassable almost immediately. They'll be lucky to move at ten klicks per hour.

"The civil response will be delayed because of the death of the internet and the struggles with anything beyond wired communications. Eventually a warning will go out through local emergency responders."

Unfortunately, Javier was right. Within minutes of receiving an alert, unmoving vehicles completely clogged every roadway. In two hours, the owners of hovercars (over half the vehicles in the area) discovered their optimism that they would glide above the waves was wrong. The ground effect fans didn't work well over water, especially turbulent water. The designers had planned for use above a hard, unmoving surface. Millions died, trapped in their cars. The military were only able to save a handful.

New Adelaide, Victoria, Australia

People gathered in droves to gape at the scene. This was what the planners had designed as a potential harbor for the relocated city. Today, mammoth piles of ice choked it.

Chapter Twelve

Seawater and flotsam were streaming back out to the rapidly receding sea. The tsunami had reached past the first seawall, destroying it.

Emily Southfield turned to Darby. "We didn't predict this at all."

Darby said, "I'll begin planning the repair of the seawall Chief."

She shook her head. "We'll let the juniors handle that Darby. We're going to want to work quickly to grab all of that ice we can. I'll want teams of people to get this all moved into the hills and buried. That will save it for the future. We'll need it."

Darby gaped for a moment. "What you're saying makes sense Chief. Guess we'll learn how to do this just as we learned how to move buildings. The only difference is that the buildings didn't disappear if we didn't work fast enough.

Emily chuckled. "Let me know if you need anything Darby. Fortunately, the spotter planes saw this coming, so we managed to evacuate all the workers. Still, we lost a lot of good people who stayed to try to save the fools who wouldn't listen to us."

Darby nodded. He was using his cyberpad to tell his crew to assemble. They would brainstorm for a half hour then divide into three teams. The first group would build roadbeds for the movers. The second group would dig pits to bury the ice into the hillsides. Dirt and rock would have to be the principal insulators for this huge a quantity of ice.

Darby turned to the chief. "Emily, can you ask the spotters to do a survey along the coast. I doubt we are the only place ice came ashore. You might want to alert New Canberra as well. This might require an 'all-hands' effort."

Emily smiled. "I was right to take a chance on you Darby. Good on ya."

Oh The Humanity

Late that day,

Lac Courte Oreilles Indian Reservation, Northern Wisconsin, USA

News trickled into Northern Wisconsin, primarily over the recently revived hard-wired telephone lines. The information was necessarily fragmented. Finally, the tribal leaders received a call over the secure lines Jay Friedman had insisted on installing. The Emergency Security Council's announcement made the disaster official. This had been far worse than the first collapse had been. Millions had died. The sea covered the entire state of Florida and most other coastal areas.

The tribal chief, John Underwood, and Sleeping Otter, the tribal Midewiwin (healer) convened a pow wow of the extended tribe. Sleeping Otter said to those who gathered. "The day we have been warned of has arrived. The earlier flood in January was simply the starting point. Today a massive wave has inundated the coastal areas. We fear a vast number have died. I suggest all pray or mourn in whatever manner you find most appropriate." The weathered spiritual leader hobbled from the stage, his spirits burdened.

Ainsley and Addison had tears streaming as they wrapped their arms around each other. Ainsley then beckoned the Scott family to join them, huddling in the cold spring air.

WHAT DID YOU THINK

OF

OH THE HUMANITY?

First, thank you for purchasing this book *Oh The Humanity*. I know you could have picked any number of books to read, but you picked this book. I am extremely grateful.

I hope that you enjoyed the book and it gave you food for thought. If so, it would please share your thoughts about this book with your friends and family by posting to Facebook, Twitter, Instagram, TikTok or your other favorite social media platform. (Word of mouth is fine as well)

Additionally, I'd like to hear from you and hope that you will post a review on Amazon or your favorite book review blog. You can subscribe to my author's blog or contact me at www.surfthesingularity.com. Your feedback and support will improve my writing for future projects.

I want you, the reader, to know that your review is very important. I read any I can find. The first review I received, from a friend, led me to a total rewrite of the first draft of the first book in this series. You can have a great impact too. I wish you all the best in your future success!

ABOUT THE AUTHOR

Daniel R Scott

Daniel R Scott is the critically-acclaimed author of the trilogy of books in the "Humanity Transformed" series. After earning a BS in computer science/math, Scott became a contributor to revolutionary outcomes of the field of IT and bioengineering Through his literary works, readers take a global voyage. They gain glimpses of his experiences, new understanding of the past, and a vision of potential futures.

Scott's life achievements have become the definition of who he is. His audacity, curiosity, intelligence, and discipline have resulted in the man, father, husband, and author that he is today. His talents enabled him to become the creator of numerous advances in IT including canonical modelling and industry standard data models, among others. He was a major contributor to the concept of master data management.

During Mr. Scott's career as an IT professional, he continually made a difference for half a century. He started as a coder and advanced to become an enterprise system architect. The systems he deployed span the breadth of human enterprise – from commerce to government to insurance, with a concentration in the fields of healthcare, biomedicine, and the environment. His involvement in multiple industries and his insatiable curiosity gave him knowledge of how things work today. His imagination and vision, guided by disciplined attention to detail, led him to create new tomorrows.

Other than being an impactful member of society, this happily married man and father of two enjoys reading every type of book, travelling locally and globally, and taking part in charity work. This is why, when he turned 60, he pedaled 6,000 km in a charity bicycle ride that raised money to support persons suffering from lung diseases.

Daniel R Scott can be described in numerous ways but at the core, he is an author by heart, soul, and profession. His love for words and a solid sci-fi epic is indisputable.

ACKNOWLEDGEMENTS

First and always to the Lovely Lois. Not only is she my first and best editor, she also wrote several parts of the book. Her name should rightly be on the cover as well. She will have to settle for half of any proceeds. Second, a special shout-out to my number one international fan, Hope from Kyogle, New South Wales, Australia. I look forward to spending time with you during my next visit Down Under.

Humanity Transformed

A post-apocalyptic history that follows people worldwide striving to put the world back together. In their attempts, the survivors edge ever closer to unleashing even greater woe on a weary world; technological singularities that threaten to render humanity irrelevant. Or worse.

Oh The Humanity

This current book is a prequel to the Humanity Transformed series fills in the backstory for some of the main characters of those three novels. It tells a few tales of the Days of Trouble that preceded the largest mass death event in history, the Great Dieback. It hints at the dramatic occurrences during the recovery period that follows. The evolution of artificial intelligences and enhanced humans threatens the remnants of humanity with destruction, again.

We follow the stories of a diverse global cast. The Cameron twins are geniuses in the fields of cybernetics and bioengineering. Hope Scott and her family are struggling to survive a rapidly changing inner-city neighborhood. Around the world, self-aware AIs emerge. The Price family endures the Australian civil war. Scientists begin providing people with superior biological capabilities.

Will classical humans, overwhelmed by recent traumas, learn to surf the singularities and survive the turmoil?

Great Dieback To Singularity

Revised January 2021. Purchase available at numerous outlets. Check www.surfthesingularity.com.

The Cameron twins were each a genius in their respective fields of cybernetics and bioengineering; Bachelor's degrees at 16 and PhDs at 20. But every time they got ready to enjoy their youth, life would send them a curveball. Then things got serious.

This is a near-future history covering the period after the Great Dieback of 2029 and spanning the world. Over half the world perished when the icecaps melted. This event triggered flooding, tsunamis, starvation, volcanic eruptions blanketing the planet in global winter, and the general breakdown of societies. By 2033, a weary world is recovering.

People are struggling to adapt to the new realities. Then the real dangers emerged. Artificial intelligences, robotics, and bioengineer-enhanced humans threatened to produce a singularity; the event where more capable creatures began evolving at an exponential rate. Human beings might become irrelevant. Or a nuisance to the new lords of the Earth. Will the twins and others fight, die, or surf the singularity?

Singularity To Humanity

Revised January 2021. Purchase available at numerous outlets. Check www.surfthesingularity.com.

The saga continues. Each of the Cameron twins continue their quest separately. Ainsley, with her fiancé, has gone to China and they link up with her ex-boyfriend Xiang. They escape a nuclear explosion and flee across the Himalayas.

Addison and her paramour lead an elite squad in pursuit of the heinous trio -- Dr. V, Count Grubby, and the Biensur Beast -- from Africa to the crippled lands of South America where the villains partner with a drug cartel.

New warriors in the fight for humanity's soul are introduced. Yasmeen and Farah Khan are taking this opportunity to tackle a small, new project – reinventing the socio-politic-economic order. They fight desperate battles against foes on all sides.

We meet the king of all of Africa who is the puppet of the demonic AI Kisasi. We meet Diana and Darby, young, unassuming Aussies struggling with civilization's collapse and the prospect of young love.

Titanic battles are unleashed on land and sea as sentient beings of all types strive to define humanity's future. Can these far-flung forces stop the creation of another army of supersoldiers and the cabal of AIs?

Last Crucible Of Humanity

Published January 2021. Purchase available at numerous outlets. Check www.surfthesingularity.com.

This is the climax of the saga of humanity's search for survival and meaning in a world where they will no longer be the sole rulers. Our heroines and heroes face the ultimate test and find their base beliefs challenged. Will they succeed? Will they still be human?

The final novel in "Humanity Transformed" is a mind-blowing read, centering on a Russian family Morizov. The book gives readers a vivid description of how the Morizov's country is overrun by desperate Chinese hordes fleeing catastrophic flooding. Worse, the Russians also experience a nuclear attack from the West, devastating the remnants of the country. In the midst of all this, the Morizov's shine a ray of hope, unveiling a secret plan that allows millions to escape the dual onslaughts.

It is a genre-defining piece of science fiction literature that ends up engaging readers on how people deployed human enhancements and artificial intelligence to aid or combat conquering armies as well as how the Russian survivors fled first one country then another before departing Earth in a final diaspora.